THE WHISPER OF
A DISTANT GOD

by
David L. Gersh

Books by David L. Gersh

Art Is Dead
Going, Going, Gone
Desperate Shop Girls
Art Attack
How to Collect Great Art on a Shoestring
Pot Luck
The Whisper of a Distant God

For my dear wife, Anne without whom my books
would not be possible. And for my late wife, Stella with
whom I began this journey.

The North and the South both knew that God smiled upon their cause. If God did take sides, it was a small blessing. Over 620,000 Americans died in the Civil War. More than in World War I, World War II, Korea, VietNam, Afghanistan and Iraq, combined. It was truly The Whisper of a Distant God.

This book is a work of historical fiction. The events and most of the main characters are real. But the psychology, fears and motivations of the people involved are fictional. I created the letters, diary entries and journals in this book, although some of the language, here and there, came from the diaries and letters of Civil War women and soldiers.

Surprisingly, almost all the newspaper articles are authentic. I want to thank Jerry Thompson for his biography of Henry H. Sibley, from which much of the information on him in this book comes.

I hope I did a good job of making these real people real for you. They are real to me.

Historical Figures

Mrs. Edward (Louisa) Canby
The wife of the Union Commander, Edward Canby, and the Angel of Santa Fe.

Colonel Edward R.S. Canby
The Union Commander.

General Henry H. Sibley
The Confederate Commander.

Colonel John Slough
The Colonel of the Colorado Volunteers and the commander of the Union forces at the Battle of Glorieta Pass.

Major John Chivington
The officer who was detached by Colonel Slough with a force of 400 men. He destroyed the Confederate baggage train at the Battle of Glorieta Pass.

Colonel Thomas Green
The officer to whom Henry Sibley ceded command of his Army of New Mexico.

Lt. Colonel William Scurry
The commander of the Confederate forces at the Battle of Glorieta Pass.

Major Charles Pryon
The second in command of the Confederate forces at the Battle of Glorieta Pass.

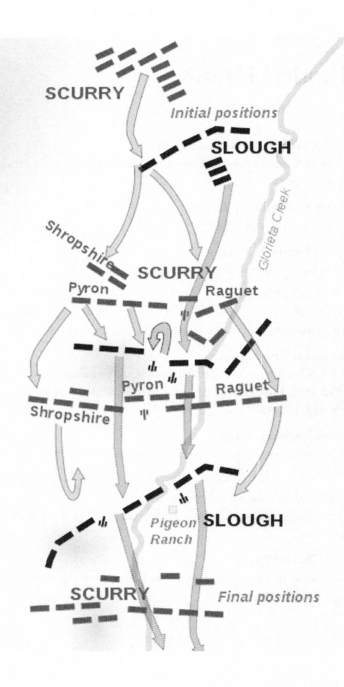

SCURRY

Initial positions

SLOUGH

Glorieta Creek

Shropshire

SCURRY

Pyron

Raguet

Pyron

Raguet

Shropshire

Pigeon
Ranch

SLOUGH

SCURRY

Final positions

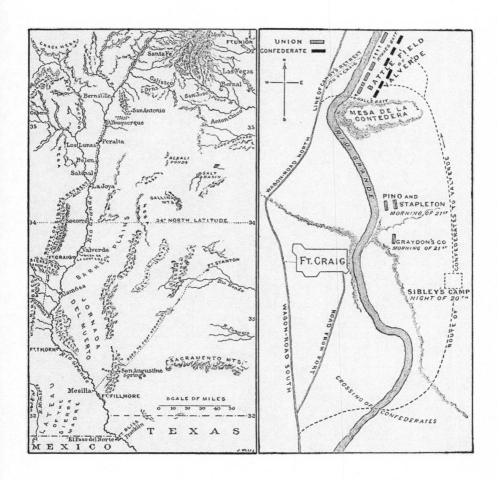

Chapter 1

Ezra Davis stood looking at the two graves, his weight resting on his right foot. A gust of wind stirred his hair.

The old graveyard stood on a hill behind a rusting fence. There were bare spots where the grass had dried up. No one was in the graveyard at this time in the afternoon.

Feelings, he thought, still ran high up here. Down in Texas too, truth be told, even after all these years. Couldn't ask no one. So it was hard to find.

The wind gusted up. It blew dirt across his scuffed shoes. A confederate gray sky leaving blue a memory. It matched the man. He was old. Not so much in years. But like the war had made him.

Gaunt, unshaven. Maybe five feet, ten inches. Eyes a watery blue. His mama always used to tease him about his eyes. "Ezra, I don't right know where you came from," she'd say, then she'd tousle his hair and laugh.

His hair was clumped down, shaggy and graying in places. Chopped up where he couldn't get the scissors right. Still showing the marks of the campaign cap he held in his left hand. He wore an old gray uniform jacket. The outline still showed where the sergeant's stripes had been torn off. The right sleeve was folded over to cover the stump of a forearm.

A bead of sweat ran from his armpit down his side. He gazed up at the sky. He knew it would rain soon. Break the heat here in Indianapolis. Strange name. Strange place.

He straightened up and shifted his balance to both feet. He needed to say what he'd come to say.

Her headstone was simple gray granite. Nothing fancy about it.

1

How she'd have wanted it. Her name, "Louisa Hawkins Canby," was carved into the stone. Beneath it, the words, "The Angel of Santa Fe."

Next to it was a larger, more ornate headstone inscribed, "Major General Edward R. S. Canby, U.S. Army." But Ezra spoke to Louisa.

"It's Ezra Davis, Ma'am. You won't remember me. There was lots of us. But I come this way 'cause I had to say thank you for what you done."

He spoke aloud in a clear voice, as if he were speaking to his Texas boys back in New Mexico during the war. His teeth were yellowed and a few were missing toward the back. He rubbed at the gray stubble on his cheek with his left knuckles.

"It was the newspaper that fin'ly brung me, ma'am." He had been there for almost half an hour looking for the grave stone. Now the stump of his arm was beginning to throb, as it did sometimes when the weather was changing.

"I was at home, done with the mornin' chores. The land 'round Austin ain't good for much. I hears a horse. Now there ain't many visitors out where I am.

"Reached for my old Sharp and looked out the window. Billy Wikkins. Hain't seen Billy for like on to two years. Heard he settled down up to the north, near Butler, with that girl he was always writin' to. Lost my Becky 'round that same time." He paused for a moment and was still.

"Well, me an' Billy, we got down to flappin' 'bout the war and what. Billy were in my company. Good man, Billy.

"Danged if he don't pull out this newspaper. Unfolded it and slapped it on the table. Said he couldn't right believe his own eyes. Billy were always one to exaggerate a bit.

"I don't read so good. But I looked right close at that paper and darned if there weren't a picture of Henry Sibley, that son of a bitch, beggin' yer pardon. Made hisself out to be some kind of hero, accordin' to Billy. And it talked about you too, ma'am. Your passin' on. I knew right then I ain't done proper by you. Knew I needed to come." He blinked at some dust that blew into his eyes.

"We'd a starved or froze back there if it ain't been for you." He remembered her leaning over him, speaking in a soft voice. Gently placing a wet towel on his forehead to try and break the fever. She was not pretty. A thickening woman, middle aged even then, her hair parted and pulled tightly back in a bun, with a motherly way about her.

Chapter 2

December 25, 1838
(Crawfordsville, Indiana)

Dear Diary,

What a wonderful birthday. Edward came for Christmas dinner and he has asked me, Louisa Hawkins, to **marry him**.

He is so very handsome. How can he love me as he says he does? I am such a plain girl. Oh, father was so pleased. I am sure he thought I would be a spinster. I did too. Goodness, I am twenty years old.

Edward is tall and upright. His dark eyes are thrilling. Imagine, me, a soldier's wife. Thank goodness Sophie introduced us. What a sweet sister she is.

I know I will be a good wife to him. He says he wants a big family. I imagine us sitting by a fire and reading with the children bustling about. I will be reading. Snow will be falling and we will be so warm and peaceful.

No, I must not be so skip-headed. I will need mother to show me better how to cook and run a house. College has not taught me any of that. Father wanted me to be able to live on my own. But now I will have a family to care for.

Edward says I must finish my schooling. He does not believe in leaving things unfinished. He is quite disciplined. And I am head-strong. I need to be careful to obey him and not be a flighty girl.

He wants us to be married when he finishes West Point. I wonder where we will be sent. It will be such an adventure. Sophie and Rupert are assigned to Washington. I don't know how I could live in such a big city. I would rather be someplace like here. But Edward says we will make do, no matter what.

Chapter 3

(Edward Canby to his mother from Jacksonville, Florida)

My dear Mother,

I know my letters are infrequent and that you must think me a wayward son. And perhaps you are correct.

But I write with grand news. Lou and I are to have a child. We were past hope, but now we are blessed. Of course, Lou is as delighted as she can be, as am I. She is a fine wife and a sturdy girl. She holds up well to our life. It is not easy here in Florida. It is an ugly, wild place, with none of the civilizing influences of Indiana. The heat and mosquitoes are dreadful. Lou stays in the small settlement of Jacksonville while I am in the field.

I am sure we will have a wonderful child. We have talked of naming him Edward if he is a boy, or Mary, after Grandmother, if a girl. Lou has spoken of returning to her family when she enters her confinement. I believe that would be wise. I would welcome your advice.

I fare well. The heat here is not to my liking. I am more comfortable in dryer weather. Apart from the swarms of mosquitoes, there are many strange reptiles. They are large creatures with armor. They look like dragons, but they are called alligators. Last week, one of the soldiers died from being bitten by a very small, colorful snake. Not at all like our rattlesnakes.

We are much in need of additional men. The recruits available are not always of the best. However, we persevere in our campaign against the Seminole. They are not as fearsome as they are made out to be. They are brave though ill equipped. My, what I could do with them if they were mine.

We carry our supplies on pack mules. They are ornery animals. Yesterday, the mules we were packing for the very first time scattered in every direction, kicking off their cargoes. Tin pans and camp kettles went rattling. Mules braying, men cursing. It formed as strange a song as one is likely to hear. We didn't recover one of the mules until today. And, Lord, the noise must have awakened every Seminole in Florida. If you had been here, I would have heard your sweet laugh again.

Do not be concerned, I am taking care to avoid harm, while still doing my duty. I am enclosing $10 with which I hope you may buy some luxuries. Please forgive the shortness of this letter. I fear your daughters would do better. But I am only a son.

I miss you. Please say hello to Pa from me.

Love,
Edward

Chapter 4

We have a daughter! We named her Mary, after Edward's grandmother. She is a healthy and happy little girl. She is beautiful. With her dark hair and green eyes she looks so like Edward. Such tiny hands and feet. I love her so.

I have never been happier, although I have little energy. Goodness, I had no idea childbirth was so difficult. Mother never told me it was painful. Perhaps she doesn't remember.

Mother and my sisters are very attentive. They fuss over me and Mary all the time. Coming home was a good decision. I am very tired. I have been up with Mary every night for the last week. Thank goodness Edward is not here or he might be upset. He does not like to have his sleep disturbed. But perhaps he would have welcomed this. I choose to believe so. He is a good man.

When I return to Florida, I will have to rely more on Bess. She is very smart for a Negro girl. But she does bear watching. What a peculiar tradition, this slavery is. Bess belongs to Captain Joseph and we hire her from him. I cannot imagine owning someone.

Perhaps Edward will be reassigned before summer. I do not look forward to another summertime in Jacksonville.

Edward writes that he will return to his regiment next week. I do not believe the Army is very effective against these savage Indians, but they continue to pursue them. Such is the Army, I suppose.

I have made a personal decision. I do not believe a woman with a child should keep a diary. That is the stuff of childhood. I am no longer a child. I now shall keep a journal only.

Chapter 5

"An angel, like it says there on your gravestone, that's what you was." Ezra Davis placed his cap back on his head. "That's what we called you. Still do." The hint of a smile twitched at the corners of his mouth. "Ask any of the boys."

Davis leaned forward and touched the grey stone gently with the tips of the fingers on his left hand. The stone was cool.

"You cared 'bout us boys. Even us Southern boys. And you, a Yankee general's wife and all. Rest only cared about them officers. That's who they remembers. Not my friends who died or would'a. Not my brother, Walter. You couldn't save him, ma'am, tho you tried. Died of the pneumonia. All that war and he died with nary a scratch. Died all the same."

He brushed a tear away from his left cheek with a quick move and spit on the ground. Then he remembered himself.

"Sorry, ma'am. Shouldn'a done that."

He turned his face and raised his right arm to wipe at his mouth. The edge of the big safety pin holding up his sleeve felt cold against his lips. A wasp snapping in the air distracted him for a moment. He shooed at it with his cap.

"They lie, you know." He went quiet for a moment. "No one don't live on in memory like they said when they buried Walter in Santa Fe. Not mine no how. Not like he were."

He thought back to other graves in open fields far from home. With men—boys actually—rolled together into scratched out graves in the hard ground. Wrapped up in blankets. They had no coffins.

Davis turned towards the other gravestone and replaced his cap. He brought his feet together and saluted awkwardly with his left hand. He'd never been very good at standing at attention. It had gotten him in trouble.

"Begging your pardon, General Canby." He dropped his arm. "You didn't beat us. Not you and all them bluebellies. Not even Kit Carson could'a. We won every fight. Good boys we were."

His eyes went vacant and his back stiffened as he remembered. Valverde. Glorieta Pass.

"Even took your guns. We was out generaled was all, damn Sibley all to hell." He focused again.

"Yes, sir." He looked back at the woman's grave. "Your lady there, she damn sure captured more hearts than you Yankees ever captured Confederate bodies."

Chapter 6

July 27, 1847
(Crawfordsville, Indiana)

My dear Husband,

I received your welcome letter today. I have not yet gotten a permission to visit you. I have applied directly to General Scott since I can find no one else to listen. I hope that is permissible. It will be a long trip, but we want to be with you. It has been a year since you left for Mexico. I miss you greatly, this first time we are parted for so long.

Mary and I continue to do well at Mother's. It has been hot here, but not as hot as in Florida. There are beautiful wildflowers in bloom. Mother is having a hard time of it since she broke her arm last month. I help her with the housework, and she sits by the fire at night and reads to Mary. You would not believe how much Mary has grown in the last year and how much she has learned. You would be most astonished.

We are proud of your promotion to captain. Please share with us what deed you performed to warrant such an honor. I am sure it was grand. The Mexicans must fear my brave husband.

Do you now command a company? Or is it a regiment? We can certainly do with more money, Mary seems to grow out of her shoes every month. But please do not worry, as we do well with what we have.

My sister Sophie is still in Washington, D.C. Rupert also has been promoted to captain. She complains that his is only a brevet promotion. Somehow, it is temporary and can be taken away. And it does not have increased pay. Isn't that unfair? Can you please explain it to me when you next write? Will we not have more money? Rupert does not like being made to stay home when there is a war to be fought. I believe he envies you.

I have a great deal to tell you when I see you. Mary and Mother join me in our love for you. May God hasten the time for us to meet. And we pray that you remain safe.

Your affectionate wife,
Lou

Chapter 7

October 10, 1848
(Monterey, California)

Dearest Mother,

I am grateful to you for allowing Mary and me to stay with you for so long a while. When Edward is away, we become sad and you made us both so happy.

At last, we have reached our destination, safe in every particular, in health and in spirit. Our possessions are as in good order as anything could possibly be after the hard journey we have had. While it was indeed difficult, we did enjoy it and the journey did not seem to last almost a month. It is a long way from Indiana to California.

Most particularly, Mary delighted in the new sights. The plains extend out forever and the land teems with buffalo. We even saw a band of Indians in the distance. Of course, with our numbers, we were in no danger. I wonder at how large this country of ours is and how few people there are in this huge land.

We had two wagons to ourselves. One in which we rode and a second for our furniture and goods. Both were covered in stout canvas so we were not troubled by sun or rain. Edward arranged for us to travel with several other families until we reached Texas where we joined with two other wagons that were heading to California. From there we were escorted by a goodly number of soldiers to keep us safe as Edward was concerned about the recent Indian problems in Texas and Arizona.

The weather was mostly fair, although we were caught in a great rainstorm in the vast area of the Texas plains. There was mud everywhere. You cannot imagine. Our wagon sank to its wheel hubs. We had to get out into that awful mud. The soldiers unhitched the mules from the other wagons and hitched them up with our mules. Even then, we could barely drag our wagon out.

Well, I needn't tell you that Mary and I were just covered in mud. You would have laughed at your rag-a-muffins. It was a whole day before we reached a river and could wash.

California is so unlike Indiana. The climate is mild, even in October. We traveled through a high desert that is different than Texas. There are huge mountains interrupting the land.

We approached Monterey, which is halfway up California, on the Pacific Coast, through lush valleys where ranchos stretch for miles and miles. What a wonder in a dry place. We saw cowboys in big Mexican hats who were herding many head of cattle. Mary jumped up and down, clapping her hands.

The wagons stopped for the night on a cliff overlooking a beach. Mary and I made our way down to the sand before it got dark. Mother, you would not believe the ocean. How vast it is. Vaster than any of the plains. It makes the great Mississippi River seem small. We were thrilled.

I dipped my foot into the water. It was so cold. Mary got too close and a big wave wetted her to her thighs, she screamed and danced before I pulled her out. She was laughing so.

It was a boon to finally be with Edward again. This was the first time we had been separated for so long a time. He will not speak of the Mexican War, but we know how brave he must have been to deserve two battlefield promotions. He is now a major.

Today, when we had settled in a little, Edward introduced me to a long thin man with red hair, whose place he is taking. Edward told me that his name is William Tecumseh Sherman. What a peculiar name. He does not look like an Indian. But he is a gracious man and quite charming.

Our house is two stories and made of adobe. That is what the Mexicans call bricks they make from clay mud and straw. It is white-washed to keep it from melting around us.

Our rooms are tidy and comfortable, having stone fireplaces that give us a general warmth and cheerfulness. I think I shall have a carpet made for the floor. There is a soldier here who Edward says is quite handy. Then, perhaps, we will feel settled.

Edward has arranged for a Mexican woman to cook for us and another to help me clean. It is so good to be in my own house again. To finally be still, in one place, where I know we will remain for at least a year.

I will close this letter now, dear Mother, as Edward will be soon returning. I wish to make sure his meal is on the table, as he desires.

I remain your loving daughter,
Louisa

November 2, 1848
(Monterey, California)

Dearest Sophie,

I am always glad to hear from you, sister, and read that Rupert and your family are well. Remind me when next you write how old my three nephews now are? I am startled at how quickly time passes and how the children grow.

Thank the good Lord, Mary is thriving. She turns seven in three weeks and will enter school when we get settled here. You well know the life of the Army.

We have been in Monterey for one month now. We are blessed. Edward and I are together again. The war with Mexico was the first time we had been separated for so long. Mary does so miss her father when he is away.

Edward received his brevet promotion to major in the war, but, of course, we will see no increase in his pay. Now, he has assumed his duties as Assistant Adjutant-General. It means he will be traveling all over the District to be sure things are faring well at all our many posts. I will miss him, but that is the life each of us chose.

This town of Monterey is large, almost 2,000 people I would guess. And there are many Mexicans. That was to be expected. There is also a large group of Chinese people. They seem very strange to me and I fret a bit over the idea that I will have to deal with them. Their skin is actually yellow and their eyes are peculiar.

Ships arrive every day full of rough men who are going to the gold fields. Thank goodness, they are in such a hurry to leave, or I would be frightened. Imagine leaving your family to look for gold. What must those poor women do?

It is cold here and it rains often, although it is much milder than it was in Indiana. We are housed in an adobe house outside of the Presidio, which is what the Spanish call a fort. It is an ample house, but rather rustic, as you would expect.

Next week, I shall undertake to get to know all of the officers' wives. As the wife of the senior officer, I fear I will have more responsibilities than I can handle.

I must look for another Mexican girl to help with the house. The one Edward found is so lazy, she makes more work for me. The Chaplain of the post is also the Schoolmaster, so I will seek him out and introduce Mary to him.

It appears that between the suttler's store—suttler is the name we give the post merchant here on the frontier—and the produce and beef brought in from the farms outside of town, we will not starve. Although, goodness knows the cost of everything is going up. I sometimes fear we shall have nothing on the table when Edward comes home for dinner. Would not that be a sight?

Write to me soon. Give Rupert and the boys my love.

Your devoted sister,
Louisa

March 14, 1849
(Monterey, California)

Dear Mother,

It has turned rainy and everything is wet and muddy. Oh, it is dreadful. Five straight days of rain. Man and beast get stuck in the mud and cannot move. It is like glue and takes a man's boots right off. A foot and a half deep. It is difficult to get about.

Mary must walk carefully on boards they have laid in the streets to get to school. They shift and slide. But my, what a beautiful school

Mayor Colton has built. A large stone building, the lower floor for the school and the upper for the town hall.

Everyone tracks mud into the house. There is no respite from the dirt, even though no one is allowed to wear shoes inside. We must clean and clean. We now have two Mexican women with us at home. Rosita is the older and helps me cook and bake. Juanita helps with the housework, but is lazy, as was the last one. I may need to find yet another woman soon. It is a constant problem. Perhaps I will try one of the Chinese women.

Yesterday, Captain Jenkins and his wife arrived. He is the second officer to arrive since we came to this post. His wife, Elizabeth, seems amiable. It is always pleasant to have new women among us. It is one of the few joys of army life.

But bless me, every time a new officer arrives, it becomes dreadful for the rest of us. Thank goodness Edward is a major and not likely to be outranked. Any officer gets to choose his house based upon his rank. So, Captain Jenkins got Lieutenant Boyd's house, even though he and his wife have no children. Martha Boyd had to pick up her four children lock, stock and barrel and move next door into a smaller house where the Monroes were living. And so on. You can imagine the fuss.

We call it "falling bricks" because one knocks over the next. It makes each of us anxious because we do not know how long we will be in any house, much less any post. Lord, if we only had known before we chose this life. But we endure with good nature.

Three soldiers deserted this week. Edward says this is a constant problem. Army life is even harder for ordinary troops and not a life for everyone. Goodness knows there is more than enough drinking and swearing among the soldiers. I am glad we do not have to associate often, but it is difficult to be completely free of them.

Katie Bowen, Martha Boyd and I have become particular friends. In truth, we are nearly all the time together. If one of us is in the kitchen sewing, we bring our sewing as well. I tell you these particulars that you may know we do not give way to despondency or allow the better establishments of our friends in the States to make us unhappy.

Sometimes, Edward and I are invited to parties or dances at a Mexican grandee's house. How marvelous to enter a huge room alight with candles, filled with music and dancing. Some of the Mexicans have lived here for many years and are quite cultured. They are more sophisticated than I would have imagined.

Last week, we attended the engagement of Mr. Stanton Burton to Amparo Ruiz. The party was at the Ruiz rancho. They own at least a mile of land above Monterey. The main house is quite splendid.

Miss Ruiz is beautiful and appears very aristocratic. She was dressed in a long white dress embroidered with white birds. Her long black hair was crowned with a lovely comb inlaid with ebony and silver. She has dark eyes and is very slim and erect. Mr. Burton made his affianced a gift of a gold necklace that ends with a large opal in the center.

Edward says she is the granddaughter of a governor of Mexico. Their engagement has been the talk of Monterey, not all of it good. Some foolish people think that it is wrong for a Protestant to marry a Catholic. The Catholic Bishop has denounced the union and the Governor is considering a ban. Well, I say pooh. They both believe in our Lord, Jesus Christ. Why cannot people stay out of others' business. It is hard enough trying to live from day to day on this frontier.

I must close this letter, as Mary will soon be returning from school. Oh Mother, you would love her so much. She grows and blossoms into a young woman with each day. And so sweet and good. The Lord has sent me a great joy.

My love,
Your faithful daughter,
Louisa

April 24, 1849
(Monterey, California)

Dear Mother,

It has now been six months since we came and this seems to be a good posting. It is not actually the frontier, as it well might be, but a real town. Thank goodness, the rains have stopped. Food is plentiful.

Venison, beef, and wild fowl come in from the ranchos surrounding us. Mexicans bring donkey loads of vegetables and fruit for sale. The Chinese offer all varieties of seafood and fish. Our vegetable garden is flourishing and we have a cow for milk.

I have even learned to churn butter. Mrs. Burton, Mrs. Jenkins, and I share a stone butter churn, a butter paddle, and an earthenware pan for working the butter. I am getting quite good at it.

Our chickens lay fine eggs. We have 10. Only sugar is expensive, $.20 per pound if you can believe it. Good gracious. And we have to get flour from the post suttler, which is a big expense. Almost $20 a barrel.

Last week, I made plum preserves. I sweetened it with molasses. Edward is fond of preserves with his toast in the morning. And he is quite particular. But he remarked how good it was, so I was pleased.

Mary is doing well at school and continues to blossom. She is pretty and sweet. But she does like to get in trouble with the other children. Were we such a trial?

We live plainly and well and have plenty of clothes. You would not imagine that we are so far from fashion and civilization. All the ladies dress very prettily. And the Mexican women sew beautifully. The ladies here wear woolen double gowns in the colder weather and then come out with bareges or some other gossamer thing.

It is a quiet place and we feel safe. The Army does not even post sentries, except over the arms and supplies. The Mexicans are very accepting of the change in government, although the richer ones are concerned. They appear to be a docile people.

We had a dance on the post last weekend. The officers' wives did all the decorating and arranging. We had the soldiers set up a big tent. Some of the younger ones provided the music. The wives baked biscuits and cakes. And there were four hams. A few of the single men ordered peaches and grapes, which were a treat. I, of course, played matron in the way of presiding at the supper table, serving coffee and, you know, what all.

I even got Edward to dance once. Now, how is that! The enlisted men were very neat and well behaved. They seemed clean and had their boots polished. They are not nearly as rough as I had imagined. It is so rare that we are with them.

Our dance came off very well. Everyone appeared to enjoy the food and the music. None of the enlisted men got drunk, as I was afraid they might. We got many nice compliments.

I hope that you are well and that your rheumatism is not troubling you in excess. Have you heard from Sophie? I have not had a letter in two weeks. You must chastise her, leaving her poor sister without the joy of her letters, while she plays. The great city of New Orleans has so much more than we have in our humble little town.

Your loving daughter,
Louisa

July 14, 1849
The Personal Journal of Louisa Canby
(Monterey, California)

Oh goodness, Edward is furious with me. I am a willful woman, I admit it. I wanted to laugh, but, of course, I could not.

I allowed Mr. Burton and Miss Ruiz to use our home for their wedding. After the Governor's announcement of his silly ban on the marriage of a Catholic to any other religion, they could not marry at the family's rancho. Given the sentiment here against the Mexicans, Miss Ruiz's uncle felt it was too dangerous a thing for a Mexican family to do.

Mr. Burton lives in a room at a rooming house so they surely could not marry there. They were so upset, and I have grown fond of Amparo Ruiz. She is a cultured lady of great dignity.

Well, Edward left on one of his short inspection tours. And Mr. Burton and his new wife are good Christian people, so I said bah to all this foolishness and offered our home to them. It was a lovely wedding, if I do say so.

You would have thought the whole world had come to an end. Apparently, the Catholic Bishop of California was simply beside himself. At least it was so, according to the newspapers. He must have been red in the face, all spitting and fuming.

What with the Governor getting onto the General, the General got onto Edward something fierce. Edward says it could have wrecked his career, which may be something of an exaggeration. The only way he got free of them was to say he knew nothing of it at all. Which is the God's truth. But he is feeling angry at not having a good, docile wife.

Well, I suppose I could have hurt his career, but it was the

Christian thing to do. Mr. Burton and Miss Ruiz are a fine couple. I think I did the right thing and hurt no one. That is what is important.

Edward is set to depart again tomorrow. He will be gone for several weeks. I need to ease him that I will be good while he is away. I shall be, I suppose.

Chapter 8

Edward Canby was in his oldest uniform, the one he wore when he was to be gone on one of his long inspection tours. It was clean, but threadbare in places. Tatters had been mended here and there. Its dullness seemed to make the gold epaulets on his shoulders shine brighter.

He dabbed at some jam on the corner of his mouth and placed the napkin on the table. His daughter smiled at him and he smiled back.

"Will you be a good girl while I'm away? And take care of your mother?"

Mary giggled. "Papa, you know I'm not old enough to take care of Mama."

It brought a broad smile to Louisa's face. "How long will you be gone, Edward?" she said, turning towards him.

"I expect to be gone no more than two weeks this time. I need to see the garrisons north of San Francisco." He frowned. "No matter what I find, there's no money. Sometimes, I wonder why I inspect them."

It was so unlike him to criticize the Army. There was a little start of concern in Louisa.

"Please take care. Somehow, I feel a bit unsettled."

"Lou, there's no need for concern. I will have six men."

"Usually, you have more, do you not?"

"Yes, but several men are sick. I can't spare more this time. But we are always cautious. Things are quiet. There is no need to fear. I'll be back safely."

He rose and stepped to his daughter and hugged her from behind. Mary gave a little cry of pleasure. He kissed her on the top of her head. "I'll be back soon."

"I'm going to miss you, Papa," she said, her face upturned to him.

Louisa rose and Edward kissed her on the cheek. She and Mary watched as he gathered his things. "Take care of my little girl," he said to Louisa, winking at Mary as he shut the door.

"Now, Mary, you need to get yourself ready for school. Hurry along now, dear."

"Mama, I feel funny. My throat hurts." Mary had just returned for lunch.

Louisa put the back of her hand to the child's face. "You do feel a bit warm. Perhaps you should stay home for the rest of the day."

"But I like school."

"I know, dear. Just for today."

Louisa put a pan of water on the fire. She mixed the hot water with honey and brought it in a mug to Mary's room. "Here, my little invalid, drink this. It will make your throat feel better."

Two days later, Mary was burning up and coughing. She had a peculiar red rash behind her ears that seemed to be spreading.

"Rosita," Louisa said to one of her Mexican women, "go to Thomas McKister and ask him please to come as soon as possible. Tell him Mary is unwell."

Thomas McKister was the post surgeon. Louisa had known him for the several years they had been posted to Monterey. A balding, stout man, he had a kind face and a calm manner.

"Louisa, it's the measles. We've had several men come down with it in the last few weeks," McKister said.

"Oh, dear."

"Now, it is usually just a passing thing. No reason to be alarmed. All we can do is wait and keep her comfortable so the Lord can do his work. Try to get her to drink as much as you can."

"Should I keep putting cold compresses on her forehead? She's very hot."

"Yes, that's fine, if they seem to help."

"Thank you, Thomas."

McKister was replacing his few instruments into his battered bag. "Louisa, I'll have Captain Putney send a rider to your husband, just so he can know his daughter is ill."

"Yes, please, Thomas. And thank you again."

Mary was making a good recovery. It had been a week. Louisa sat reading to her after dinner. Mary just loved to be read to. She was such a bright little girl.

Louisa looked up at a small sound. Mary seemed to be having trouble concentrating. Her head dipped. The doll she was holding slipped from her fingers.

"Are you all right, darling?" She reached over to the small side table and poured cool spring water into Mary's glass, then rose and held it to her lips.

"Do you want a drink of water, my pretty one?" Louisa murmured, gently brushing Mary's hair aside. Mary shook her head, no.

"I feel so sleepy, Mama." She said, her eyes closing.

"Sleep well," Louisa sighed, falling back into her chair. Her own exhaustion finally caught up with her and she nodded off too, still holding the glass of water.

A few hours passed. Then Mary shuddered and gave out a small cry. Louisa lurched from her chair, instantly awake in the flickering lamp light.

"Mary!"

She called again. "Mary!" There was no response.

The glass she was holding shattered on the floor as she lurched from her chair towards the bed. The small huddled form under the covers lay still.

Louisa threw herself upon the child. She felt no movement. She hugged the child to her. She fumbled with the covers with one hand, trying to hold Mary and touch the girl's chest and face. The child's brow and cheek felt cool, not warm. She shook Mary, gently at first, then harder.

"Oh please, no. God. Oh please, no".

Her throat tightened over a bellow of pain. This could not be. No, it could not. Tears ran, coursing down her cheeks, wetting the bodice of her night dress. She rocked the child, sobbing, muttering again and again, "Please."

She stared at the still, small body, willing it to breathe. She stared at it for an eternity on her knees beside the bed, holding Mary's hand. Then she fainted.

Louisa was very cold. The fire had burned out. What was she doing on the floor? Then she remembered. The cry started deep in her chest and tore through her. The wail she emitted tore her soul. She pounded the floor with her fists.

"No, please God, no." The words rasped from Louisa's throat. "Let me die too. Please."

The next morning, Rosita found her there, tucked into the corner beside the edge of the bed, still sobbing uncontrollably between hiccups. There were shards of glass on the floor. Blood oozed from cuts on Louisa's hands and feet and stained the wood.

Rosita brushed aside the shards and fell to her knees. "Madre de Dios," she exclaimed. She didn't notice the sharp cuts to her own hands. Louisa stared off into space and wouldn't respond to the lady who was kneeling before her, holding her in her arms.

Chapter 9

September 18, 1849
(Monterey, California)

My dear Mother,

Forgive me, but I have no one else. I feel as if you are the only one who can understand my pain. I am alone. All of the officers' wives have been so caring. Yet it does not ease the pain inside of me. I cannot eat. I cannot sleep.

It has been a week now since we buried our dear Mary. She was such a sweet child and so joyful. I am looking at her little dolls as I write to you.

The measles took her quickly, thank the good Lord. My heart breaks still at the memory of her little face. Oh, mother, my tears are staining this letter so I fear you will not be able to read it.

Edward has finally returned. Our message failed to reach him in time for him to say goodbye to his daughter. She was not even ill when he left. His first question upon returning was "How is Mary?" Edward is a good soldier, so he is unable to allow himself our feelings. But I can see in his eyes and in his manner how he is torn inside. He did love her so.

I know that you are not able to make the long trip to be with me. Nor would I want to have you do so. But knowing that you are there for me is so important. I shall go on, for there is no other course.

I must stop writing now.

Love,
Louisa

Chapter 10

December 6, 1849
(Monterey, California to her sister)

Dear Sophie,

I am quite annoyed with you. I have not heard from you in a
month, although I have sent you three letters during that time, which
I hope you have received. None the less, I thought I should write to
you and give you and Rupert my wishes for the holidays. I do pray
that your family is well.

Now that Rupert has been posted to New Orleans for some time,
I would ask to know how you find it. It would be difficult for me, I
think, to live among the Southerners and their Negro people. But
then, you have always been of a better temperament than I.

We had a Thanksgiving dinner, although I did not feel much like
giving thanks this year, may the Lord forgive me. I miss Mary so.
However, Edward felt that we must do it. It is expected that the senior officers will have a dinner for the younger ones on this holiday.

We had Captain Jenkins and his wife Elizabeth, as well as Martha
and Jacob Boyd who I have told you about. Katie Bowen also came
with her husband Augustus. There were several children. Oh my, that
made it difficult. It almost ripped the heart from my chest.

I think Edward was proud that I did not show my hurt, particularly in front of our guest, John Fremont. Captain Fremont is staying with us while he attends a political convention here in Monterey.
They are discussing applying to the government for statehood, I believe. I am not sure why that is important, but it does sound so.

Does Rupert know Captain Fremont? He was at West Point

while Edward was there. It may have been before Rupert's time. Captain Fremont is a big, blustering man, so full of himself he could burst. We had no choice but to offer him a bed, given Edward's connection to him. You know I am a forthright person, and though it may be un-Christian of me, I do not like the man. He is a trial every day, always expecting to be waited upon and not a thank you on his lips.

It was indeed a good Thanksgiving dinner we got up. There was roast beef and a fricasseed chicken, as well as some veal. I made potatoes, turnips, and onions. The wives brought mince pie and I made a cake. Edward was able to get some wine, although you know, I do not drink it, as well as some porter and ale. It would have made folks stare to see all the empty bottles, but with all his coaxing, Captain Fremont could not get me to take a drop.

I think all enjoyed themselves, as we could not get them out of the house before 8:30 in the evening. Thank goodness it had not rained in several days or the house would have been an even greater mess. It will be a job to clean up, I tell you.

I think of Mary every day. But every day passes, and I do what I must. Write to me soon.

Love, your devoted sister,
Louisa

January 8, 1850
(Monterey, California from Edward Canby to Henry Sibley)

Dear Henry,

I write now because you expressed interest in this new California in your last letter. And Louisa and I, to my great surprise, turn out to be at the center of the storm. General Riley called a convention here that has now concluded. He had to call a convention. Our do-nothing Congress in Washington did just that, nothing.

What with the gold rush, there are now over 100,000 people here, if you can believe that. We could not let California drift. There are too many Mexicans. Even with the Treaty, it is getting to be a problem.

The delegates were pretty much a motley bunch from all over the state. Politicians mostly. Many were so mean with their money, they didn't take lodgings, but camped outside under the trees. We had Johnny Fremont staying here with us this last three months.

Remember him from West Point? He still is everything he was then, but more. Always in the right place. Now I understand he got rich off California gold, just by blind luck. At least, that's what Bill Sherman said.

Not an easy man, Johnny, though he may make something of himself one of these days. As a politician, I warrant, not a military man.

Lou was really riled to have him with us so long. But maybe it was good for her to get so angry. Since Mary died, she has been real quiet. Well, let me tell you, she wasn't while John was here. He rubs her wrong. She thinks he is loud and silly. Nearly tore my ear off complaining. But John did tell me all that was going on at the convention.

He was saying all the time how hard he was working, but maybe they got somewhere. California is not even going to be a territory first. They wrote a constitution and are trying directly for statehood. Lou and I think that is grand and we intend to do what we can to help, my duties permitting.

They have decided California will be a free state and have said so in the constitution. That will stir up our old arguments, but I still think I'm right. I just don't think we should allow slavery to spread into more states. I have no love for the Negro. But it is not right.

I am leaving again on a tour of the eastern garrisons. Being Adjutant-General is hard duty and I would rather soldier. You are fortunate. At least when you have to leave, it is with some purpose. You get to fight the Indians. I just look and see and report. Nothing ever changes.

Maybe they'll reassign me soon. The only good thing about Monterey is the weather. It never gets really cold. I remember that night in Mexico when we were camped in the mountains. You had gotten in from patrol and you were just about frozen through. You cozied up to the fire. Just a little too cozy as it turned out. Caught your coattail on fire. You danced around that fire, beating on yourself like some kind of whirling dervish. I still laugh recalling it.

Well, I hope we meet again soon. Please convey my regards to

Charlotte. I trust that all remains well with your family.

With respect, your friend,
Edward

February 16, 1850
(Monterey, California)

Dear Mother,

Yesterday, the ground shook so that I thought the roof would come down on me. I was very frightened, never having experienced anything like it. Gracious, this would never happen in Indiana. Of course, Edward was not here. He is off inspecting posts and garrisons in the east of the Department.

There are many cracks in our walls that will have to be mended. I have asked Sergeant Willis, Edward's aide, to see to it. I believe he can, but I cannot know. He seemed certain enough.

We are fortunate. Several buildings in Monterey fell down and there were eighteen people killed. Mrs. Boyd, Captain Boyd's wife, was knocked to the floor and injured her arm. Mrs. McKenzie was out in the street and was almost struck by a falling brick.

I hope we do not see more of these. They come without warning, I am told, sometimes much worse than the one we had. It is frightening to think of. At least, if there is a tornado, the sky darkens and there are signs so you can get to the cellar. There is no place to be safe in these so-called earthquakes and no time to prepare or pray.

Both of our Mexican girls seemed to take all this much more as normal. Apparently, they have experienced several of them. Let the good Lord spare us any more while we are here.

Many of the Chinese women and a few men were out in the streets, giving the most awful shrieks in their strange sing-song language. You might have believed the world was coming to an end. Several of their rickety wood houses collapsed and caught fire. Our voluntary fire department rushed to help, not so much for the Chinese, I think, but to prevent the fires from spreading. The Chinese are looked down upon in Monterey, almost as much as the Mexicans.

Things have returned somewhat to normal today and I did marketing and set a fire in the oven so we can bake bread. Edward is to return tomorrow and I want him to have a fresh loaf. He always complains about the Army bread when they have been riding hither and yon for weeks. But I believe he actually likes being away.

He seems silent here with me sometimes. Perhaps it is the melancholy I have felt since Mary died. I fear I am not so good a companion. I do try, but I cannot be what I am not. I also fear that I am becoming old and unattractive. Life has been hard here.

Winter is upon us again, but here it is not very cold. It has not rained nearly as much as last year. There are still a lot of vegetables brought into market and the Chinese always have fresh fish. They do all the fishing. It is their trade. We will not starve. This is a land of plenty.

As always, I worry about your health and hope that you remain well. I fear that I will not be able to return home this year. We may be reassigned. It has been two years. And that will take all my time and energy.

I still miss my dear Mary, particularly in the evenings when Edward is gone. Pray for me.

Please express to all of my sisters my love when you write to them. And I send my love to you.

Your faithful daughter,
Louisa

May 18, 1850
The Personal Journal of Louisa Canby
(Monterey, California)

Jacob Boyd has been promoted and posted to Fort Union in New Mexico. Yesterday I took a walk into the countryside with Martha Boyd where we saw beautiful pansies and foxglove of every hue and color. It will perhaps be our last walk, since they are to leave next Friday and there are many things Martha must do.

How well I know the burden upon Martha and her family. There will be no help from Jacob, of course. Katie Bowen and I will help, but with Martha having three children, it will be a task. We will do our best to ease her burden.

She is very excited, but also apprehensive. Fort Union is a much wilder place than Monterey. Jacob will command a company of mounted troops. The Indians are still hostile in the Territory and he will certainly see fighting. I think Edward is envious. He is so bored with administrative duties.

Goodness, who shall I adventure with if not Martha. She is more spunky than I. It was she who started talking to the Chinaman who sells us fish, the last time we were in town.

We never would have seen the flag he received from China otherwise. It was eight feet wide and four feet broad, of the nicest crepe. It was crimson and had an immense dragon upon it, wrought with gold. Enormous eyes gazed at the moon. It was the most magnificent flag I have ever seen. Mr. Woo was quite proud of it. He offered us tea, but even Martha was not brave enough to accept. And to think I found the Chinese unsettling when we first came. They are just people.

We have been at this post for almost two years now. I would be happy to leave. The memory of my dear child still haunts this house. But, of course, I have no say in the matter. The Army will do as it always does. My husband is an old soldier and understands perfectly the management of all things connected to the Army.

I have asked Edward if I might go visit Sophie and Rupert in New Orleans. I have not seen my sister in three years. He says it is not a good time to go, but I will discuss it with him again. He is a good man, but he tends to be stubborn, and watches his coins carefully. Well, I do also. I have saved enough from my household money to make the trip.

It has turned mild and the rain has stopped. I believe it will be dry for the rest of the year, judging by last year.

There is great excitement about statehood. Edward and I will help as we can.

We have settled in here. I have a vegetable garden, so we do not have to buy vegetables at any price they ask. We have fifteen chickens that give us eggs. And our cow produces all our milk. I am becoming good at making our butter, as it is expensive. Some of the commonest things are richly priced, even in this land of plenty. The cost would buy us luxuries in the States. But I am making do.

My only want is enough books to read. Edward is not much of a reader, but I devour books like he would devour a well-cooked steak. I have written Sophie to see if she could purchase me some books in New Orleans. But she is not the most attentive writer, and I have yet to hear.

September 2, 1850
The Personal Journal of Louisa Canby
(Monterey, California)

It has happened again. I awoke to the silence. It is so hard when Edward is away. My bedclothes are damp with sweat. I am exhausted. I fear to sleep.

I dreamed of Mary again. It has been a year. Will there be no respite? Please Lord, comfort me. I beg you.

September 19, 1853
The Personal Journal of Louisa Canby
(Monterey, California)

Edward has been short-tempered all week. He is often this way when he has a cold and cannot pursue his duties. This cold has been particularly heavy and he coughs a great deal. He was forced to cancel a review of the garrisons north of San Francisco. How he does fret.

I understand, but frankly, sometimes, it becomes difficult for me also. Of course, I do not show my unhappiness. It is not my place. Fortunately, I seem to have the constitution of a mule. And be as stubborn as one sometimes, or so Edward says.

We did receive pleasant news from the Army. Edward has been confirmed to the permanent rank of major. His brevet rank carried no increase in pay, but now we will receive $12 more a month. Goodness knows, I can put the money to good use.

Even with only the two of us, sometimes, it seems impossible to keep our home together. The drought has caused my garden to dry up and the price of vegetables and meat to increase so much I can scarcely put food on the table. Edward is oblivious to my problems. He is a man.

We have been ordered to remain here in Monterey and Edward is to continue his role as adjutant-general. They say it will be for the foreseeable future. He does not complain, but I know that he chafes at others being in combat, if only with the heathen Indians. He feels he is idling away his career in the shadows and has no opportunity to distinguish himself or rise in the Army.

The drought has caused awful problems for our friends, the Ruizs. It has gone on for two years now. We hardly have had any rain. And what we have had are referred to here as gully-washers. It rains very hard for a short time and runs off before it can do anything to relieve the drought.

Many cattle have died and those that have not, have been sold off at low prices. It seems that Senor Ruiz will have to sell most of his land to pay his taxes and feed his family. It could not be a worse time to sell. At least, in that sense, we are fortunate to be in the Army, with all its silliness and problems.

I went yesterday to Mary's grave and placed flowers on it that I had dried last summer. It was the fifth anniversary of her death.

Lord, will it ever be easier? I fell to my knees and sobbed, as weak as some newborn. My dress got all dirty, but I did not care. Katie Bowen is the only one of my old friends still here. We are very close, and I can talk to her about Mary. She too has lost a child, but she has two others.

Friendship is so difficult for me. Edward has his friends from West Point, but we wives must always make new friends. Just as we feel close to someone, it seems that they are gone.

Well enough of my caterwauling. I will make Edward a hot rum and perhaps we can read by the fire and not have words.

Chapter 11

December 16, 1855
(Henry Sibley to his wife from Fort Bridger, Utah)

My dear Charlotte,

I am reminded again how difficult it is for me to prosper in the Army. I fear it attracts only dull and unimaginative men who are unable to recognize more than the petty limits of Army duties. I do not mean to complain, but I find myself irritated by my commanding officer's lack of insight. He speaks to me in a disrespectful manner and it is all I can do not to respond in a like manner. However, I will continue to persevere and deal with my obligations.

I have submitted to the Army my designs for the new tent I have shown you. I also have applied for a patent. People here are referring to it as the Sibley Tent, which pleases me. Many officers recognize the unique qualities of my design and have written enthusiastic letters to accompany my submission.

I believe that this will greatly benefit the service and that we may finally have some relief from our financial distress. I confess that our growing debt has weighed on me greatly. I hope to hear from the Army soon, but as we know, it moves slowly in making decisions, even those that should be apparent.

Please try to return as soon as you believe possible. I pray that your sister is recovering well from her indisposition. I do miss your counsel and comfort. There are so few in whom I feel I can confide.

I have had another attack of stomach pain. The doctors do not know the cause. The doctor advances the thought that it may be caused by kidney stones but he has no cure. I am dealing with the pain as best I can.

We leave tomorrow on yet another attempt to curb the Indians. I shall be unable to post a letter to you for some weeks, so do not fret. I regret I cannot include any money for you, but in truth, I have none. I think of you often and remain

Your faithful husband,
Henry

Chapter 12

August 8, 1857
The Personal Journal of Louisa Canby
(Fort Bridger, Utah)

President Buchanan has ordered the army to march against the Mormons. Edward says the Mormons have raised a mounted militia they call the Nauvoo Legion. What a peculiar name.

I am, of course, concerned, but Edward says the Army will make short work of these untrained fellows. I do so hope he is right. But he is pleased to once again be soldiering after so many years in Monterey.

New-York Daily Times

No. 7 | New York City | August 8, 1857 | Vol. 1

The Official Report of the United States Judges in the Territory of Utah, as made to the President has been published. The hostile and seditious sentiments manifested by Governor Brigham Young are the reason for the withdrawal of the Judicial Officers from the Territory

The Report, signed by all three judicial officers, details the malpractices of Governor Young and his followers. The Government of the United States is shamefully spoken of and ill-treated and Governor Young indulged in sundry maledictions upon the memory of General Taylor.

The Report proceeds to comment upon the prevalence of polygamy in the territory. Plurality of wives is openly avowed and practiced under the sanction and in obedience to the direct command of the Church. The evil can never be made a statutory offense by the Utah legislature.

The Great Salt Lake is an important Overland route to the Pacific, but emigrants avoid it. No man can open his mouth in opposition to the lawless exactions of the populace, with safety of his liberty, business, or life.

This gross violation of our principles cannot be allowed to continue and must be dealt with by force, if necessary. We call upon President Buchanan to right this wrong.

"Charlotte, I do not think I can abide these people longer."

The fire flickered, its light licking at the walls and ceiling. Charlotte and Henry Sibley were settled in deep, scuffed leather chairs. Their faces were in shadow. The shadows danced across them.

Charlotte clutched a shawl tightly around her shoulders to ward off the drafts. No one could seem to properly seal the house. God knows, she had tried. It was perpetually cold. Henry seemed impervious. Perhaps because he spent so much time outdoors.

Henry was shaking his head, his lips squeezed into a frown. He held a tumbler of whiskey, from which he was sipping. The glass caught the light as he moved it back and forth to his mouth. Dinner dishes remained soaking in the pan behind them. Henry had needed to talk.

"This Utah Expedition was hopeless. We had no leadership." The Army had finally returned from the last expedition against the Mormons. It had not been successful.

"St. George Cooke despises me. He sees me as a threat to his authority."

Charlotte nodded and reached for Henry's hand. There was no reason to speak.

"He is such a small man," Henry finished, taking another sip from his glass.

He was quiet a moment. "Can you imagine. He berated me in the vilest language for not signing my muster rolls. Muster rolls. I did not have time to do so. The man had demanded them immediately. All this paper work is nonsense, in any case."

"I am sure you are quite right, Henry. He does seem to have a grudge against you."

"The man used totally inappropriate language. Very unbecoming. Of course, as a matter of conscience, I had to respond. He accused me of drinking. By God, I drink less than he does."

Charlotte had been concerned for some time about Henry's drinking. It had been increasing. But this was not the time to address it.

Henry was visibly getting more agitated. His hand was shaking. A dribble of whiskey slipped down the side of his glass to the floor. "He intends to bring me before a court-martial. An outrageous charge. Charlotte, what am I to do?"

"It will turn out well, dear. Do not become so upset. You are in the right. They will see that."

"There are so few opportunities for me to express my ideas. The Army is so limiting. Perhaps it is time to resign my commission. We should think of returning to New Orleans. I am sure I can earn a good living there."

Charlotte noted that his voice lacked conviction.

"It is certainly something we should consider," she said. "But what would you do?"

"There must be many things I can do. Banking or perhaps trading in cotton. I understand that is quite lucrative. I might work for the railroad."

"Those are excellent ideas. But we must not be precipitous, Henry." Charlotte was concerned about many things, particularly the stability of her family. Henry had never done anything but serve in the Army. He disliked paperwork. And he had a fiery temper, more pronounced, she believed, due to his drinking. She got up to stir the fire. The sparks brightened the room momentarily.

She turned and spoke softly.

"I am certain this court-martial business will be resolved. Then we can consider our course. You are a smart man, Henry, and a good officer. They will not humble you."

Henry raised his tumbler and took a longer drink. He stared pensively into the fire for a long time.

Chapter 13

Henry Hopkins Sibley was indeed a proud man. He came from people with a distinguished history of military and civilian service, stretching back to the earliest days of America.

John Sibley sailed to Salem, Massachusetts, in 1629. Timothy, Henry's great, great grandfather, rose to the rank of Lieutenant Colonel for his service in the Revolutionary War.

In Louisiana, Samuel, Henry's father, amassed a large estate, leveraging his position as the Parish Clerk of Court. Samuel built a stately brick mansion in Natchitoches, on sprawling acres of land. The house was set on a rise, a few hundred yards from the Red River and he called it Court Hill.

Little Henry Sibley was born in 1816 to Samuel and Margret. A plantation in the South was a fiefdom, the slaves its serfs. Henry was the young princeling.

His childhood was spent amid tall pines and stately oaks. Steamboats plied the Red River. The whistles were easily audible and tantalizing to the boy at Court Hill.

He grew up in the luxury of the plantation, rich and secure. His father was an important man and his uncles were even more important. Some of them were famous. His uncle Josiah Stoddard Johnston, the half-brother of General Albert Sidney Johnston, became a United States Senator in 1823 and was a close friend of Henry Clay.

The army was becoming an ever-increasing part of the Louisiana frontier. In a South steeped in a long attachment to military tradition, the spectacle of soldiers parading was mesmerizing. Henry had a lot to treasure.

Then, when he was only seven, his world crumbled. Samuel died of a kidney ailment in 1823. As tragic as Samuel's death was, the full repercussions were yet to unfold. It turned out that Samuel had mortgaged the family properties and run up massive debts to fund his passion for real estate speculation.

Henry's mother, disturbed and angry, faced an ever-increasing group of creditors, loudly demanding payment, as she struggled with the family's financial insecurity. The bitter struggle finally ended on March 15, 1826.

With emotions running high, Margret and her humiliated children watched as their possessions were auctioned off in public. Court Hill, its land, and all its beautiful furniture were gone. A family of position and fortune was reduced to nothing. They were poor. The blow was shattering. They had to leave.

On a cold winter day they all boarded a steamship bound for St. Louis to live with Margret's brother, George, and his childless wife. George wrote to his brother-in-law, Senator Johnston, "It is my purpose to do the best I am able for them all. Henry is (a) promising boy for his age. I shall put (him) in school ..."

Margaret, at the urging of Senator Johnston and Uncle George, decided that fourteen-year-old Henry should attend the Grammar School of the University of Miami at Oxford, Ohio.

Miami was a light in the midst of an intellectual wilderness. Richard Hamilton Bishop, its president, brought in some of the most educated men in the country, including William Holmes McGuffy, to teach.

Henry rose at 5:00 a.m. every day. Study was rigorous and the school enforced strict rules of discipline. Daily religious attendance was mandatory, as befitted a school founded by a Presbyterian minister. It was enough to crush the spirit of any teenager. Nonetheless, Henry excelled at his studies.

A few weeks after graduation, on October 19, 1832, Henry applied to the United States Military Academy at West Point. The family spared no effort to bring its still important influence to bear.

While he waited, Henry worked as a clerk in a small store in Grand Encore. It was the only job he could get. But how demeaning it was to an educated and intelligent man, as Henry considered himself.

Nor could he understand why his appointment had not been approved. He was qualified, surely. Dr. Sibley, his grandfather, had written directly to the Secretary of War. He had emphasized Henry's connection with Senator Johnston. And three Congressman from Louisiana had written a joint letter to the Secretary. Even General Henry Leavenworth had asked that he be accepted.

It was Impossible. And unfair.

Henry waited anxiously for the call. And he waited. No word came. He was determined to live up to the hopes and aspirations of his grandfather and right the wrongs done to his father, but he was being thwarted. And he fretted.

1832 wore down to 1833. Finally, in April, Henry's uncle, George, discovered Henry's appointment papers in a side drawer of his desk, where they had been placed by a house slave and forgotten.

Within days, plans were well in hand for Henry's departure to New York and his career as an Army officer. The future was finally upon him.

Chapter 14

August 24, 1858
The Personal Journal of Louisa Canby
(Fort Bridger, Utah)

Edward told me today that our friend, Henry Sibley, was acquitted at his court-martial. Goodness, I did not even know it was happening. Edward says he was charged with insubordination to a superior. To my view, his commander, Philip St. George Cooke, is far too self-satisfied, as his name would suggest. So, it does not surprise me that they should disagree. But how it came so far, I do not know.

Edward was forced to sit on the court-martial board since he is a colonel and the commander of the Tenth Infantry. Even though he knew Henry at West Point and there might be a bias, there are so few senior officers here, he was required to sit. But he so does detest these military squabbles.

Thank goodness, Edward returned safely from the expedition against the Mormons. He laughs about it. No one was killed. In fact, according to Edward, hardly a shot was fired.

He recounted to me an amusing story. It seems that the Mormon strategy was not to fight, but to deny the Army supplies. Their cavalry constantly attacked the Army's baggage trains. Since the Army lacked cavalry, the Mormons were successful.

The Union Colonel, Alexander, became so enraged that he mounted 100 of his men on mules. It seems they were called the "Jack-Ass Cavalry" by the officers. I believe they were being funny. In their only encounter with the Mormon Nauvoo Legion they were so cautious that the only casualty on either side was a Mormon cap.

Edward will not criticize Colonel Alexander, but he does not praise him either. Edward complains that the Army never even entered Utah. The advance was so hesitant that they had to go into winter quarters due to a heavy blizzard in the mountains. Before spring, the issues were resolved by the politicians and the entire expedition was a waste.

I do so wish we could be removed from all this anger over what people believe, although I am shocked that the Mormons approve of a man having more than one wife. According to Edward, one wife is more than enough.

I look back on our seven years in Monterey with some regret. The countryside was beautiful and the weather was so much milder than it is here. We now are truly on the frontier. However, it seems this very isolation brings the officer's families closer. Abigail Picman, Captain Picman's wife, has become my particular friend. Yet I find myself thinking of how temporary my friends are and how soon they, or we, shall be moving on. Somehow, it is different with the men. Perhaps the bond of service is stronger than that of mutual experience.

It is at moments like this that I miss having a family around me. I do so long for my beloved daughter. The feeling grows in me that caring is the greatest good a person can possess.

But Edward is far happier being in command of an infantry regiment. His time as adjutant-general was too long and he often thought it would be the end of his military career. Rupert, Sophie's husband, resigned his commission last month to open a store in New Orleans. Edward has often thought of resigning, but he was never certain of what he might do if not to serve the Army. He is a strong and competent man. I have no fear that he would do well at anything he set out to do. Yet, I do not believe he really wants to leave.

Tomorrow will be a busy day. We need to bake bread and churn butter. I wish we had a better laundress, for the one appointed to our regiment is simply dreadful. I do not know whether she is incompetent or uninterested. But the clothes come back wrinkled and, in some cases, damaged. I have spoken to Edward, but he says there is nothing to be done. The laundresses are chosen by the seniority of the regimental commanders and we are far down the line. We take what we can get.

Alas.

January 4, 1860
The Personal Journal of Louisa Canby
(Fort Bridger, Utah)

It has only been six months since Edward has been appointed to command Fort Bridger and has been promoted to colonel. Why does it seem like forever? Fort Bridger is little more than a wooden stockade and log buildings. The work is crudely done.

Our log cabin, however, is well-caulked and cozy. It was rebuilt just two years ago. The Mormons burned Fort Bridger down to keep it from the hands of the Army. I suppose some good must come of these foolish wars.

There is no culture. The music the men make is very simple. The dance we gave was surely nice, but somehow, it did not have the liveliness we had hoped. Perhaps the mood just was not upon us. Or it might be only me.

There was plentiful meat. The men go hunting every week and the hills are full of game. We did bake cakes and pies. Vegetables and greens are hard to come by, and expensive. There is almost no fruit other than wild berries.

The weather in Utah is cruel. It has been below 5 degrees now for three days. Still, we make do, and the wives of the officers provide comfort to one another. As the wife of the commander, I must see to the happiness of the other families and I do my best. I do need to be more careful and reserved now. It would not do for me to seem to prefer one wife over another. But I like most of them. They have chosen a hard life and some of them are very young.

The holidays were quite cheery. The Sibleys invited us to their home for Christmas. I did not tell them it was my birthday, but Edward and I celebrated secretly at their dinner. We were like school children hiding a secret and giggling over it. What must Charlotte Sibley think?

She has a very powerful personality. Charlotte is full-figured and must be five feet, four inches tall. But to see Henry respond to her, you might think she was a giant. And not a very good tempered one at that. Her house is run with a firm hand. We arrived at four and dinner was promptly at five, after the men had only one drink.

The food was good and well prepared. I do not know how the Sibleys obtained their Negro cook. I certainly cannot find one.

We exchanged gifts after dinner. I received a lovely pair of soft leather gloves, although, heavens, I do not know when I will use them. Henry gave Edward a grand Bowie knife. I believe he is still grateful to Edward for his support in all the trouble he had in his court-martial. The Sibleys go back so far with Edward, and indeed, with me. They are good friends.

Chapter 15

DEPARTMENT OF ORDINANCE
UNITED STATES ARMY
Washington, D.C.

February 16, 1860
Major Henry Sibley

Sir,

This letter will inform you that the Department of Ordinance has accepted your offer to license to the Army your patents for a tent capable of housing up to twenty soldiers and the related tent stove specified in Patent number 14,740 (to be referenced hereafter as the Sibley Tent). The license to be granted is to be exclusive and perpetual.

Commencing on the above date, you will be paid a royalty of five dollars for each Sibley Tent produced under the aforesaid license and a royalty of one dollar for each tent stove so produced, payable semi-annually. You shall be responsible for payments to all and any other person who may profess a claim to such royalty or any part thereof.

Any questions you have should be addressed to the undersigned.

William M. Weekins
Colonel
Department of Ordinance

Chapter 16

August 18, 1860
(Fort Craig, New Mexico)
The Military Journal of Colonel Edward Canby

We have surveyed Fort Union. The buildings, with scarcely an exception, are rotting down. The majority are scarcely habitable. All of them would require substantial repair if they are to remain in service. The troops live in tents for lack of quarters and the hospital, commissary, and quartermaster's building are entirely unfit for the purposes for which they are required.

These times are uncertain. There is more and more talk of secession. That could lead to war. Many here support the South. I have therefore ordered that a new fort be designed and built. I have selected Captain Glover, of my former unit, to design and oversee the construction. I perceive it will be a star fort in shape with ditches and earthen breastworks.

My belief is that this fort, with its position on the Santa Fe Trail, will become the center of materials and provision stores for the Department. I believe it will be efficient and defensible. We must entrench to be able to resist a far superior force.

I have dispatched Captain Glover to Taos and Abiqui to recruit such Utes and New Mexicans as we may need to assist. Time is of the essence. He has been ordered to purchase the additional flour and beef to sustain the new men and their families. He is also ordered to provide them with cooking utensils.

There will be 200 men working day and night on the entrenchments and breastworks. I anticipate that in three weeks, the fort will be defensible. Work can then commence on the quarters and storehouses. I further expect that the new fort will become fully ready within forty-five days of today's date.

Chapter 17

PERFORMANCE REPORT
Brevet Major Henry H. Sibley
September 30, 1860

Major Sibley has been adjutant of the 2d Dragoons since January 1, 1860. I have had the opportunity to work closely with him and to observe his conduct.

He is well spoken and presents a soldierly bearing. He is a brave soldier.

Unfortunately, Major Sibley has shown a disposition towards irregularity in carrying out his orders and has exhibited a lack of organization that I deem necessary to the performance of his duties. Nor has he exhibited the initiative expected of a senior officer. This may be attributed to his excessive consumption of alcohol, which has become more pronounced than previously noted in his Performance Report.

He is intelligent, but excessively irritable, leading to a lack of compatibility with his fellow officers, and occasionally to actions bordering upon insubordination to his superiors.

Major Sibley cannot be recommended for promotion at the present time. He will receive a copy of this report.

> Colonel William McIde
> Commander
> 2D Dragoons
> United States Army

Chapter 18

May 4, 1861
The Personal Journal of Louisa Canby
(Fort Craig, New Mexico)

It has been chaos here. We have learned that Fort Sumter in South Carolina has been attacked and many of the Southern states have seceded. Edward explained to me that secession means that they have withdrawn from the Union. He says it is because of slavery. Well, the Negros are not people whom I would choose to befriend, any more than the Chinese or the Mexicans or the Indians, but why is this something to fight over?

I asked him why secession was different from the colonies quitting the British. He did not explain but I seemed to have angered him. He said it simply was.

Officers have resigned their commissions. Many fine men have left to join the Confederacy. Edward says that even General Lee has resigned. He turned down command of the Union Army to return to Virginia. I cannot understand how an officer's loyalty to his state can exceed that to his country.

Henry and Charlotte Sibley are leaving. Henry was born in Louisiana. He, too, is loyal to his Southern roots. We are losing good friends. It saddens me to see our Country so torn and I fear for us.

There is talk of war. I cannot imagine us fighting and killing men with whom we have lived. Who have been our friends. Perhaps, here in New Mexico, so isolated from the States, there will be no war.

How odd this all is. Everyone is thinking of something else. Messengers come galloping in all hours of the night. The soldiers are unsettled. Companies are losing their officers through resignation and being assigned ones strange to them. Edward has always said that to have an effective army, the officers must know their men and the men must learn to respect their officers.

Edward seems to be coping. He is a simple man, but strong and steady. He has a calmness about him I can never hope to have. In the midst of this, he is trying to organize an expedition. The Apaches have raided a settlement near Taos and massacred many of the people. What savages they are.

I will need to gather food for us. We do not know what will happen. The officers' wives, at least those who are staying, are very concerned. There is no feeling of fear. Just uncertainty. It is my responsibility to calm them. We are all concerned for the children. Edward says everything is safe and we will be well. I pray he is right.

Chapter 19

As the Southern states began to secede, the people in a portion of the New Mexico Territory, now southern Arizona, were known to be almost unanimous in their support of the South. In a convention held in Tucson, they formally annexed their part of Arizona to the Confederacy, and elected a delegate to the Confederate congress.

Settlers in the area felt betrayed by the government in Washington, who had ignored their pleas for more protection from the Indians, surveys to ensure their claims on the land, and effective law enforcement.

The Weekly Arizonian
(Tubac, August 1861)

Since the withdrawal of the garrison troops, the chances against life have reached the maximum height. Within six months, we predict nine-tenths of our people will be slaughtered. We are hemmed in on all sides by the unrelenting Apache. The whole male population will have been killed off, and every ranch, farm and mine in the country will have been abandoned in consequence.

The mass of people in the rest of the New Mexico Territory, most of whom lived in the Rio Grande Valley, were largely apathetic in their attachment to the Union. Indeed, some of their territorial officers were bitterly opposed to it. California had a strong element that sustained the Southern cause. One third of the settlers in Colorado were openly or secretly disloyal.

It also was believed among those in the region that, if given the opportunity, the Mormons of Utah would heartily support the enemies of the Union. Several warlike tribes of Indians in the Southwest also could be incited to fiercer hostility against the Army. There was good reason for the Confederates, Henry Sibley among them, to think that a rebellion in the West was possible, if not probable.

There was one problem, but no one thought it was important, if anyone thought of it at all. The Republic of Texas had invaded New Mexico twenty years before, in 1841. The invasion was a commercial and military expedition to secure the claims of Texas to parts of Northern New Mexico.

The expedition was unofficially initiated by the then President of the Republic of Texas in an attempt to gain control over the Santa Fe Trail and further develop the trade links between Texas and New Mexico. The initiative was a major component of an ambitious plan to turn the fledgling Republic of Texas into a continental power. It had to be achieved as quickly as possible to stave off the growing movement demanding that Texas be annexed to the United States.

The Texans had already started courting the New Mexicans, sending out a commissioner in 1840. Many Texans thought that the citizens of New Mexico might be favorable to the idea of joining the Republic of Texas.

They were not. The invasion was a fiasco. The Texans were captured and held prisoner. Many New Mexicans had a long memory and a bad taste, even twenty years later. It would impact the co-operation the Confederacy needed and expected.

On February 1, 1861 Texas seceded from the Union and began at once to recruit troops to occupy the forts within its own limits and those in New Mexico.

The nearest Union fort in New Mexico was Fort Filmore. Lt. Colonel John Baylor of the Texas Volunteers marched on it on July 24, 1861.

Fort Filmore was about 6 miles from the town of Mesilla, near the Texas and Mexican border. The fort originally had been built directly on the Rio Grande. The river later changed course, leaving the fort a mile from the river. This forced the Army to use water wagons to supply the post with water and made it hard to defend in the event of attack.

Baylor led 300 men from Fort Bliss, Texas, forty miles up the east bank of the Rio Grande. They, however, brought no artillery.

The Texans reached the vicinity of Fort Filmore at night and placed themselves between the fort and its water supply at the river. But Baylor canceled a planned attack after learning that one of his men had warned the garrison. His Texans then forded the Rio Grande and early that afternoon entered nearby Mesilla, a strongly pro-Confederate community.

With 380 infantry and mounted riflemen, Union Major Isaac Lynde approached Mesilla from the south on July 25. He sent an officer to demand the Confederate surrender.

Baylor rejected his demand, and Lynde ordered the attack. After three Union enlisted men died in a bungled charge and two officers and four other men were wounded, Lynde retreated back to the Fort Filmore. The Confederates suffered no casualties.

Baylor sent to El Paso for artillery and additional men. When Major Lynde discovered that Baylor had sent for artillery, he ordered Fort Filmore abandoned.

The retreating Union soldiers, suffering from thirst and exhaustion, were approached by 300 Confederate soldiers. Major Lynde surrendered his 500 demoralized troops without firing a shot.

It was an embarrassment for the Union. And it encouraged Henry Sibley in his belief that the Union Army, in the Territory of New Mexico, lacked courage and leadership and would be defeated.

Chapter 20

It was raining. It always rained in Richmond, Virginia, at this time of year. Three days now.

Mud stuck to shoes and wagon wheels and invaded every home. It fouled the carpets in the well-appointed rooms in the Monumental Hotel, directly across the square from the great state building built by Thomas Jefferson. Richmond had been named the capital of the Confederacy the preceding month. No offices were ready yet.

In a suite in the hotel, three men sat at the round table in the flickering light of the candles. Jefferson Davis had never liked the smell of kerosene. A blazing fire danced shadows onto windows streaked by tears of rain.

Davis had always been thin, but he had lost more weight in the last fortnight. He seemed unsettled. His strong jaw worked the muscles of his smooth face. As he opened his mouth to speak, he was interrupted by the stout man sitting across from him. "We should at least hear Sibley out," he said.

They were distracted by a tap on the door. "Come in, Issac," Davis shouted. He was angry. He didn't like being interrupted and he didn't like the stout man. But he needed him.

The servant entered carrying a tray with a bottle and three thick bottomed glasses. "Put it on the table there," Davis said, gesturing at the black man towards a small side table.

"Yes, suh. Will you be needin' anythin' else?" Davis made a dismissive gesture with the back of his hand.

He picked up the bottle of amber liquid. "Good Kentucky Bourbon," he said, pouring some into each glass and passing them out. "Little enough comfort in this damned rain." He tipped the glass to his mouth. He swallowed and felt the burn in the back of his throat.

"You know," Davis said, staring directly at the stout man, "they have found only six rolls of copper wire in all the South. We have no place to make muskets. Hardly any to make cannons. There are no gunpowder mills. I don't know what we're going to do. Every city wants to be defended." He ran his hand through his thick hair. "Lee's a good man. But he needs arms. The Union Army is massing near Manassas."

"We ain't got enough soldiers," said the quiet man who had not yet spoken.

"I know that," Davis snapped. "I didn't want this war. Damn it, I didn't even want this job."

They had heard this all before. Davis rubbed at his blind eye without noticing. He leaned away from the fire and rested his head on the back of the high chair. He sighed heavily. It all seemed so futile. They just didn't see.

"But, Mr. President, this plan Sibley is proposing will cost nothing. And think if it could be true. The silver of Colorado and the gold in California. A port on the Pacific. It could change the entire war."

Davis lifted his head off the back of the chair. "What do you know about this Sibley?" His voice was resigned.

"He was regular army. A major stationed at Fort Union in New Mexico. He was a good Indian fighter."

"Is he another one of these glory-seekers?" The fire was smoking a bit and he coughed. "Open that window a crack, will you," he said to the quiet man. "Lord, I'm so tired of having to listen to fellows like that," he continued. "Seems like everyone wants a piece of my hide."

The stout man spoke again more quietly, putting down his tumbler of whiskey. "The peace commissioners you sent to Lincoln were rudely turned out." The stout man paused to sip his whiskey. "The Union wants war, not peace. We need to do something. This Sibley's from Texas. He knows the West."

The stout man placed a hand on the table and leaned forward. "He says the whole territory is ripe for the plucking. Men will flock to us. Sibley thinks he can easily raise a brigade of Texas boys. It would be a great stroke against the Union."

"And he wants to be a general."

"Well, yes," said the stout man. The stout man reflected that Davis was getting testy.

Davis rose from his chair, rubbing his back. "This weather," he complained. He paced the room. Both of the seated men remained silent. They had seen him like this. His hollow cheeks were reddened by the fire. He rubbed his hands together, as if to warm them, as he paced.

"What Sibley says makes sense," the stout man said to Davis's back. He knew he was pushing.

"We need so much," said Davis, turning. He looked worn out. "We can't spare anything."

"Sibley says his men can live off the land. The people will help them. He's not asking for anything but a chance."

"When do you see him again?"

"Tomorrow," said the stout man.

"All right. You make the decision. I'll do as you recommend. But, he gets nothing."

Chapter 21

August 8, 1861
The Personal Journal of Louisa Canby
(Fort Craig, New Mexico)

Edward has been promoted to full colonel and chosen to lead the 19th Infantry. He has also been given command of the Department of New Mexico. I am proud of him. His long-held dreams of recognition have been fulfilled. However, he worries at the cost. The responsibility weighs upon him.

More states have seceded. Texas is the latest. It appears likely now there will be war and that we will be involved. We are aware from newspaper reports and what we have observed that there is a good deal of Southern sympathy throughout the West.

War would be a terrible thing, particularly between friends. I know soldiers look upon war as a way to promotion and glory, but even the little I have seen of it is horrible beyond words. I am shocked that the cloak of civility is so thin, and so easily rent. Sometimes men seem foolish beyond words.

I pray for our country, its people, and for Edward. May God protect us and let these differences pass.

August 12, 1861
(Fort Craig, New Mexico)
The Military Journal of Colonel Edward Canby

A Texas militia of only 300 men has taken Fort Filmore and forced the surrender of a superior force of Union soldiers. It can only give comfort to the Rebels and rouse their spirits.

I have ordered the work on Fort Union to be redoubled. It must be defensible and fully manned immediately. Although there does not appear to be any immediate danger, this fort is critical to the Department of New Mexico. Fort Union is the central source of supply to the entire Department.

It is also the primary source of defense for the supply trains coming from the East. There have been reports of Texas troops moving north from Fort Stanton. The trains from Fort Leavenworth are exposed if they come by the most Southern route of the Santa Fe Trail. Their disruption would disable us.

New Mexico has raised a regiment of mounted militia, such as it is, which they have put at our disposal. These men must furnish their own clothing and equipment, though they are not paid for their service. As a result of their destitute condition, I have had to direct that they be issued supplies from our already overburdened stocks. The men are untrained and poorly disciplined. I have no confidence in their capability to stand on an open field of battle between fixed forces.

Therefore, for the time being, I intend to order Lt. Colonel Kit Carson and four companies of his New Mexico Volunteers to provide protection to the supply trains. Absent the appearance of a large force, this should be sufficient. He will rejoin me if it becomes necessary. As a precaution, I have ordered the women and children in Fort Union be sent to Mora and Las Vegas.

I have today also ordered reinforcements to Fort Craig, which lies across the primary route of attack for any Confederate force intent on attacking Santa Fe and Fort Union. I will assume personal command of Fort Craig.

General Halleck has ordered a majority of the regular army troops available to me to be transferred to the East. I have requested that this transfer be postponed given the rising threat to us. I still have received no response.

Chapter 22

September 19, 1861
(San Antonio, Texas, from Henry Sibley to his wife, Charlotte Sibley)

My dear wife,

I am working day and night to prepare for this great endeavor. It is at the sacrifice of my health, but it is a sacrifice I willingly make. I will fulfill the honor done to me by President Jefferson Davis and achieve historic things, in spite of the obstacles placed before me. Yes, my dear, even in our Confederacy, there are obstacles. Alas, it reflects a basic defect that exists in some men everywhere, I fear.

Recruits are appearing and their training is progressing as I would wish. It is taking somewhat longer than I had anticipated, but I am certain our boys have the patriotic zeal required to fill our needs.

However, I face a problem with providing them arms and clothing. The weapons from the Federal arsenals I expected and was promised have been dispersed elsewhere. Yes, the boys bring their rifles and shotguns, but these are of every type and sort. It is difficult to find ammunition and parts, even for these weapons.

I am most disappointed that Governor Edward Clark has not provided as efficient cooperation as is desirable. I cannot understand such men. He has not been at all effective in ordering men to our ranks. I fear he may be favoring others. I have had to resort to placing advertisements in Texas newspapers. While I am certain the boys will respond, it has delayed me.

Nor is there a superior officer here to whom I can look for assistance. The Departmental commander has removed himself to Galveston. If I had not taken on the tasks of recruiting and arming my brigade, in addition to all the other responsibilities that burden me, I am sure the entire winter campaigning season would be lost to me.

Bless the ladies such as yourself. They have collected blankets, quilts, flannel shirts, socks and other items. Many of the boys who volunteer are almost destitute of clothing. I, myself, was unable to find a saddle. I was informed by an ordinance officer that he was not authorized to sell any saddles. It is quite beyond imagination. If not for the intercession of a friend, I do not know what I would have done.

The citizens of Texas and the Confederacy expect great things of the Sibley Brigade. With the help of God, we will fulfill our glorious destiny.

I have received a letter from the Union Department of Ordinance. As I expected, they have refused to pay me the royalties due on the Sibley Tents they continue to manufacture. I will not take out a patent with our new country. I recognize our financial needs, but I believe it is my duty not to further burden our cause. I am sure you agree.

I miss you and the children but my small needs cannot stand before the needs of our great Confederacy. I remain,

Your faithful husband,
Henry

Chapter 23

"Sure ain't as we expected."

"Ain't, by a long shot, Ezra," Hesper Evans said.

Four months ago, I'd been up on my Pa's roof when Hesper, he comes by, all excited.

"They's recruitin' in Austin."

I ast him how he knew so much, him fidgetin' down there on his old bay horse. Hesper ain't much to look at, scrawny and snaggled tooth, but he has some book learnin'. Least more than me.

Not that I made no girls take no notice. Weren't no girls anyway. Ceptin' Becky, who was kinda special. I seen her at church. Ma's big on church. I been courtin' Becky a little.

"Heard it from Jasper Siggs. He seen it in the newspaper." Hesper hitched on the reins to hold the horse still. "I'm gonna go enlist. Be more fun then ever was."

Well, I'm up on Pa's roof, as I says, and maybe half done. Take me another day ta finish. Dang.

I says, "Hesper, you wait a day 'til I get this here roof put on and I'll go with ya." Didn't even think what Pa would say, I was so stirred up.

Hesper, he like frowns. "Well, I don't know, Ezra," he says. "I don't wanna miss my chance to bag me a Yankee. This fight'll probably be over in a month. Them Yankees won't fight when they sees we're right serious-like."

"Hesper, we been friends fer a long time." I was right annoyed. "We should do this together, you hear me. Why, you can't find yer way to town without me pointin'. One day ain't gonna make a hoot of a difference." I wanted to get my licks in to, and I'd feel a lot better with Hesper there.

Well, Hesper and me, we got us a ride on a wagon, rode us to Austin. My brother, Walter, he was with us. When I tol' Pa I was enlistin', Walter says he's agoin' too. Pa would be left alone with the chores, so I was kinda hopin' he'd put his foot down.

But Pa, he says, givin' us a hard look, "I'm opposed to it, but as it's here, you boys is doin' the right thing."

Ma, she pipes up and says how I gotta see to Walter. I don' want no part of it, Walter bein' her favorite. But she takes on to wailin', so here I am, stuck with Walter.

Anyhow, we got ourselves to Austin. Biggest city I ever seen. Musta been two or three thousand folks, bustlin' here an' there. Kinda scary, bein' so big.

Started to ask folks how we should enlist, but no one knew. Lots of boys aroun' who wanted to enlist. Me and Hesper, we was kinda worried we might miss out. Boys we seen had equipment of one kind or t'other. All we had were our old shotguns and some pots and pans. Walter, he dain't even have a gun.

I'm a leader, so off I goes to a tavern to ask how to enlist. I hear some men discussin' the war. They says a fellow name of O'Brian is formin' a company.

I says to them, "'Cuse me, but can you tell me where Mr. O'Brian is residin'? I'd sure like to join up, me and my friends."

Well, the men stops talkin' and one of them looks me up and down. Made me a little nervous. Then one of 'em says to t'other, ugly-like, "These here country boys ain't got no manners." But then another one, he says, "Oh, go on Sam, tell him where O'Brian lives, he wants to fight so bad." Then he offs and guffaws.

Well, I tell you, I was about to haul off and give 'em a piece of my mind, but I held back 'cause I really needed to know about this O'Brian fella. So I says, real nice, "I sure would like to know, Mr. Sam."

Sam, he were a rough lookin' feller. Had a squint eye too. Old cuss. Musta been thirty. He looks at me, then spits a brown stream of tabaccie juice on the floor. I wait, tryin' to look pleasin'.

Sam, he says, all grumpy, "You go west 'til ya'll get out of town a mile. O'Brian's got a brown house off to the right. Ya'll find it if you keep yer eyes open. Now get out." He shooed me away like a dog. But I hot-footed it out of there and we done set out.

We walked along. The wagon we hitched a ride in was long gone.

It was dang hot an' we didn't bring any water. Fin'ly come upon a man sittin' on his horse, lookin' at some cattle. "Mister," I says, "you know O'Brian?"

Says as how he's O'Brian and what did we want. Told him straight out we heard he was formin' a company an' how the three of us wanted to enlist.

"So, where you boys from?" he says. "You don't look familiar."

We couldn't reckon how anyone could look familiar in such a big town, but we told him honest-like.

He shakes his head. "Well, I want me boys from Travis County, so I don't rightly know if I should let you enlist with me."

I says, "Mr. O'Brian, we is three of the best boys you'll ever find. And we promise to listen to what you say and do what you tell us." I always had a ready tongue, my Mama used to say.

"Do you boys have any equipment?"

"We got these here shotguns and some pots and pans. Mama give us her bible when we're getting ready to leave."

"It ain't much, but you seem like good boys." He gives us a toothy kinda smile. "So I'll take you on, I suppose." He leans down and shakes my hand. "Let's go up to my house so you can give me your names and sign my book."

So we got ourselves in, but we didn't know what it was about. Walter, Hesper, and me was so excited, we hardly got a wink of sleep that night, what with sleepin' in a pasture an' all. We go down to town the next day to this big buildin' and get swore in.

We signed up fer three months. Figured that'd be more'n enough. Bunch of other boys signed up, mostly country boys. Few slick lookin' fellers from the town signed up, too.

Chapter 24

We was told to get ourselves down by the stables at sunup 'cause we was goin' to camp. Get ourselves trained. Hesper, he didn't feel he needed no trainin' to shoot Yankees. He says, "Just let me loose on 'em. I just hope they don't outrun my buckshot, tryin' to escape."

I gotta say, I sorta agreed with him, but I says, "Hesper, I'm right surprised at you. You don't know nothin' 'bout soldierin'. We gotta learn to march and take orders and such." I learned all that from my Pa when he talked 'bout the time he served, back when. I felt pretty smart, seein' that Hesper was better book read than me.

There was about 100 of us boys, shiftin' and stamping our feet. O'Brian, he stands up in front of us, his beard aflutterin' in the breeze. He was shrugged up inside a cape with gold trim. I guess you get cold when yer old.

"Boys, here's how it is now. Gonna provide each of you with a horse. That horse belongs to the Confederate States of America, so you take good care of it or I'll sure have yer hide." He weren't givin' us no uniforms, and that was right disappointin'.

"We're gonna be riding about forty miles west. There's a river there and were gonna be settlin' there for a month or two so you boys can be made into soldiers. Now go over there to Mr. Wickens and he'll give you three days food. You fill up any bottle you got with water. Mr. Wickens'll assign you a horse and ya'll make your mark on his paper. You boys are lucky to get a horse and saddle, you hear. Be ready to ride in two hours. Dismissed."

We did all that. The horse I got was older than me and 'bout as slow as molasses. But gentle. We could get on.

We rode ourselves to this camp. Was nothin' but a bunch of men lollin' round. Some of 'em had tents. I was hopin' someone would give me one, but no one did, so we ended up sleepin' on the ground. They give us a blanket what was none too thick. It were right rocky, I tell you. And cold.

We was told to divide up into groups of six and that's how we would eat. Called it a mess. Well, it sure was. Me and Hesper and Walter, we got us three more country boys, but we didn't know the first thing 'bout cookin'. Like on starved to death afore we got the hang of it.

Next mornin', 'bout sunup, old man O'Brian starts bellowin' at us. Had us line up. We weren't all too good at it. Then he divides us up and makes a bunch of lines, one behind the other. Another man was standin' with him we didn't know.

O'Brian, he says, "Men, this is Sergeant Babbott. He is gonna teach you how to drill. Now drilling is important, you make no mistake. You gotta learn to follow orders."

Well, I tell ya, I know'd I said that, but I sure didn't like to hear it. We told O'Brian we would listen to him, but that was to get ourselves in. I was as good as anyone and didn't like the thought of bein' told what to do. Judgin' by the look on Hesper's face, he didn't like it much either.

Well, heck, we didn't have any uniforms or nothin'. But it was our lot, I guess, so we give in.

Right flank this, left flank that. None of it made no sense. And it were dang cold out here by the river.

On about the third day, we was marchin' this way and that. Babbott took to cursin' me 'cause I was slow doin' what he said. No man's gonna cuss me, so I took after him. Hadn't been fer Hesper and Walter, I woulda like to kill him.

O'Brian, he was mighty upset. He blistered me with his tongue somethin' smart. Tell the truth, I was kinda ashamed of losin' my temper like that and I says so. Calmed him down some, but he still said I had to be punished. Made me march an extra hour every day and gave me two weeks of guard duty.

Seems like Hesper and me was always in trouble. We wasn't good with the discipline. But Walter, he took to it like a pig to slop.

Food weren't bad, but we suffered a might with sickness. The worst, I guess, were the measles. I got 'em. They sent me to a tent they called the hospital. At least it was warm. Nice lady looks after us. I lay there a few days, just burnin' up. Took whatever they give me.

Got to feelin' better, but I got me a powerful itch. Showed the doctor my long red marks of itch. He said it'd go away. Well, it didn't and I just lay there itchin'.

I get released and I'm talkin' to Willie Grimes. He's one of the boys who signed up when we did. Told him 'bout my itchin'. He says that ain't no itch, its body lice. I was rather harsh with him, him thinkin' that I was some kinda filthy person. Prides myself on keepin' clean. Ma made me take a bath every month. 'Sides, I never seen no lice.

Well, I lay down, ascratchin' and I catch something in my finger nail. It was alive, 'cause I saw its legs workin'. I was up on my feet lickity split and looked down at my hand and there were a full grown louse right there in front of me. I pulled back my bedding and seen I was well supplied with them.

We had a good fire goin' and I held my blanket and my clothes up to the heat. Cooked the hell out of 'em. But the varmints in the seams was little changed.

That night I slept but little and the next day I took all my clothes over to the hospital laundry. Told the Negro woman I wanted her to boil my clothes; they was lousy.

She says in a loud voice, laughin', "Law, child, boilin' won't kill 'em."

Thought 'bout buyin' new clothes, but I dain't have no money. So them louses and me just gotta get along.

Chapter 25

We got on to 'bout four weeks in that camp. That was when old man O'Brian announced we was gonna elect company officers. Says he is runnin' fer Captain since he raised the company. Seemed fair to me an' the boys. Got hisself elected and named the company the O'Brian Rangers, which we thought was a bit much, but shucks.

Four boys from Austin was nominated fer Lieutenant. City boys. I weren't so sure I wanted to be led by no city boy, but weren't no others put up. So we hada choose two of 'em.

Well, those four boys set about electioneerin' somethin' fierce. We coulda eat ourselves dead on election cake and got ourselves hugged into heaven by our most particular, eternal an' dear friends. I never dreamed I was so popular an' fine lookin' as I found out durin' them seven days.

So we voted, an' Bolling Hall an' Otis Baker got themselves elected. Damned if them other two din't up an' quit the company. Made me wonder how good this election thing was.

Somethin' like a week later Captain O'Brian, he calls us together an' says his wife has made us a flag. Gonna give it to us tomorrow fer which we should put on our best clothes. Hesper, Walter an' me, we got one change of under britches an' two shirts.

Next day, we puts on our cleanest and we gets lined up. Mrs. O'Brian weren't much to look at, but one of them other ladies who come along with her was good fer the eyes. Had brown hair an' 'bout no waist. Been a long time since we seen a woman. I looks at her during the whole speechifyin' and it sure made it better.

Mrs. O'Brian, she holds up this flag, had the stars an' bars in the corner. White shiny material, I ain't sure what. But it had lotsa gold braid, with the name O'Brian's Rangers stitched in the middle.

She talked real educated, 'bout the flag bein'"the proud emblem of our young republic, and how for those fated to die." Well, I tell you, I weren't gonna be one of those, but she goes on, "this moment brought before his fading view will recall kind and sympathetic words."

Captain O'Brian, he takes the flag from her and then he makes a speech. I coulda done without that, but I guess that's what captains do.

Finally, he says we is goin' to meet General Sibley in El Paso and will have the honor of takin' Arizona and all of California fer the Confederacy. Seemed like a lot of takin' to me. So I was hopin' General Sibley would have a lot of men to do it.

Next morning was clear an' cold. Walter was snufflin' and coughin'. Boy always had a weak chest. Gettin' colds an' such.

Sergeant rousted us at sunup, goin' around kickin' at the boys. Stayed away from me. Growled, but didn't come close.

Lots of noise in camp as wagons is bein' loaded and horses bein' saddled. Mules braying. Men cursin'. All kinda stuff.

There was a bugle call an' Captain O'Brian, he come ridin' up. "Men, you will be issued uniforms and equipment this morning. We'll proceed in formation to El Paso at two o'clock. I expect everyone to be prepared to move along."

I admire a man can sit a horse like him. More'n I can say fer Lieutenant Bolling Hall. No horseman him. A sorry looker, I tell ya.

Turns out I only get a jacket and mine hung down a sight in the sleeves. But no one ain't ever given me a jacket. And this one was warm too. Got a Bowie knife. Two feet long and real sharplike. Hesper, he got hisself a pistol he sticks in his belt.

I says, "Hesper, you ain't never shot no pistol. Hell, yer more likely to shoot me than some damn Yankee." Well, he ignores me, but I gotta watch that boy.

We hunted around an' got some more equipment. Didn't steal it, but it were lyin' 'round unattended where they stored the stuff. I got me a pistol too. And got us some more clothes an' blankets.

Nothin' much happened on the way to El Paso, 'cept two boys got hurt when their horses got spooked by a rattlesnake or somethin' an bucked 'em off. They was asleep, I 'spect. Now me, we was too close to our baggage train to sleep, what with all the noise an' dust.

El Paso weren't nothin' to speak of after Austin. Little adobe houses and a few hundred folks, mostly Mexicans. We come up to a fort and someone says it's called Fort Bliss. There were a powerful lot of soldiers campin' an' walking around there. More of 'em than I could ever imagine. An' there we waited fer General Sibley.

Chapter 26

December 14, 1861
(Fort Craig, New Mexico)
The Military Journal of Colonel Edward Canby

We have been warned of Southern spies surveying us. Based on the considerable threat existing, I have made a determination that Fort Union is essential to securing the Department under my command. Its strategic position on the Santa Fe Trail, in the plains between Missouri and Santa Fe, renders it critical for our defense and supply. I have requested a delay in transferring the Army forces ordered East from my command until volunteers can be raised and trained. I am awaiting word from General Halleck. I believe such depletion of our forces here, at this time, would be a grave mistake.

On my previous orders, Utes and New Mexicans have been hired to assist in the rebuilding and to perform scouting duties. We must determine the whereabouts of the enemy and harass him.

I have assigned 600 men to Fort Union. Captain Chapman reports that the earthen works and the breastwork are finished and are ready for occupation. He appears to be making good progress in the construction of barracks and storehouses within the enclosure. All public property will be moved from the old fort as quickly as possible.

Governor Rencher has resigned the Department and left for the States. He is a Southerner both by birth and inclination. At my orders, he was furnished with transportation and a military escort across the plains.

I have been required to authorize the troops in New Mexico to arrest citizens suspected of being Confederate sympathizers or spies. The arrest of David Stuart and J.R. Giddings have been effected. I believe them to be Confederate spies. They are to be brought to Fort Union for trial and have been imprisoned there.

In my judgment, the military situation is becoming of deep concern. The forces of General Sibley that are massing in Texas are still undetermined in either scope or objective. However, General Sibley commanded Fort Union briefly. Based upon my experience of him, I believe it will be a focus of his efforts.

Chapter 27

Me an' Wilbur Winkle, along with our sergeant, Virgil Smidt, was sent out foragin'. That's like stealin', but it's okay 'cause we says so. Winkle was a big fella, good lookin', but mean as a snake. He'd hit ya as soon as say hello.

Never understood boys like him an' I didn't like bein' out with him. Made me kinda jumpy. Virgil's okay, but a bit big fer his britches since they made him sergeant.

So we rides out a goodly way from camp and we sees a farm. Weren't much, but got some trees around it. Nothin' out here in New Mexico.

We been still getting some food from El Paso, but ain't enough and the boys was hungerin' fer some fruits and vegetables. Don't know why there were none, but that's the way it was.

So Sergeant Smidt, he tells Wilbur to get hisself down to that farm and inquire 'bout buyin' some stuff. We gives a note fer anythin' we buy. Ain't sure when it'll be paid.

Sergeant winks at Wilbur an' says, "Some drinkin' whiskey too, if they got it."

Now, Wilbur ain't no more polite then my dog can talk. If I was pressed, I'd wager on the dog. We sees him ride up and a Mexican fella comes out. They is jawing fer a while, then Wilbur, he hauls out a pistol and shoots the fella, just like that.

Well, I can tell ya, that created a heck of a ruckus. Two other men and a Mex woman come flyin' out of the house and the men has shotguns.

Ol' Wilbur, he takes off like nothin' I ever seen, agallupin' t'wards us, his arms flappin', the Mex's firing them shotguns at him. Sarge an' me, we turn tail and get goin' in the opposite direction from that farm. Fin'ly we rein up in a clump of cottonwoods, 'bout a mile away. Wilbur, he comes riding up careful like. He's got a tail fulla buckshot and he's catterwallin' to beat all get out.

"I's shot. Ya gotta get me a doctor."

Sergeant Smidt, he says, "Why'd you go and shoot that Mex?"

Wilbur makes like he don't hear.

The Sarge, he repeats hisself, only louder. Then he says, "I tol' you to ask them folks, not go shoot no one."

"Well," Wilbur says, "that fella was back-talkin' me and I didn't care fer his ways."

All I can tell ya is we got no fruit and vegetables and sure didn't get no whiskey. Wilbur could hardly sit his horse fer some time and done got what he deserved, I reckin'.

Chapter 28

I was bein' quiet like, you know. Doin' my spyin' business. I sure do have some luck. I don't think Sarge likes me much, 'cause I'm smarter than him.

There's a full moon, so I was crawlin'. Only scrub bushes in this here desert. Makin' no noise, 'cause I am real good. There was a sentry 'bout a hunerd yards to my left. Weren't too hard to spot caus' he was smokin' a pipe.

I was tryin' to get close enough to the Yankee camp to see what the wagon train was about. Maybe we could get some horses or somethin'. I got no inklin' whose idea it was that we should live off the land. Hell, ain't no land around here. Just desert. We ain't been grand fed, I tell ya.

I tied my horse 'bout a half mile back. Real hot fer January, so it weren't too bad. Problem was, 'round here there weren't no cover. I had crawled a darn long ways.

Well, I stopped to rest a bit. You know, listen and get my position like. There weren't no other sentry I could tell.

So I crawls around this bush and damned if there weren't the biggest rattlesnake I done ever seen. And being a Texas boy, I seen a few. Must have been six feet long and thick around as my wrist. He weren't no happier to see me than I was him.

Well, the Yankee sentry was facin' in the other direction, asmokin' his pipe. Which was good seein' as I didn't want to tangle with that snake. One thing, we boys do know our snakes, and this were a meanun.

So, I scooched back a bit and stood up, real quiet like. I took me one step backwards, and dang me, if there ain't another one a rattlin' away.

Well, I figured quiet were't getting me nowheres, so I lit out of there like my tail was on fire, jumpin' bushes and runnin' like all get out.

There was a shout behind me, but I just ran faster. A bullet snapped, but I was runnin' so fast none of them bullets could catch me. I heard lots a voices an' more bullets started comin' in, but I was getting smaller in the distance, I figured.

Must a been ten minutes 'fore I slowed down. I wouldna then, but I left my breathin' 'bout a quarter mile back. I was scooched over, tryin' to find it.

Looked 'round and listened some. Tweren't nobody close by. Problem was my horse weren't neither. Took me nigh onta two hours to find him. That horse, he looked like he was havin' a grand old time. Better'n me for sure.

Weren't the best day doin' my spyin'. And the Sarge weren't too happy neither. Still don't know what those Yankee boys is doin'. But I'm back settled by my fire and I tell ya, I intend to stay there.

Chapter 29

February 1, 1862
The Personal Journal of Louisa Canby
(Santa Fe, New Mexico)

We have made the long, cold journey from Fort Craig to Santa Fe. It has taken over a week. We were escorted by three companies of troops under Captain Wilson. We saw no Indians or Confederates. I believe the children suffered the most. They were terrified to be so quickly uprooted. I did my best to comfort them.

Edward made the decision to move the officers' wives and children with the approach of the Rebels. He is naturally concerned, but I would have preferred to remain with him. He would not hear of it. I am afraid I made him quite upset.

He has become sullen and short. He does not speak to me of military matters. Yet I gather he is not content with the volunteer forces he has. I have often found him brooding late into the evening. He anticipates Fort Craig will be attacked at any time. It is a strong place and well defended. However, Edward will not chance our staying. It is so strange that Henry Sibley is now our enemy and has set out to do us harm.

Santa Fe surprises me. It seems at least twice as large as Monterey and is certainly an improvement on the frontier posts we have seen. The main street is wide and bordered by many two-story buildings of wood or adobe. There is a large and impressive Catholic church that commands the end of the main street. Commerce appears to be quite developed. I suppose that should not be a surprise to me since it is the end of the Santa Fe Trail. But I never thought of it.

The streets are teeming with every manner of people. I see tame

Indians, Mexicans, and white folk. Even a few Negros. I suppose it is not a God-fearing town, there are so many saloons.

We have been put up in two large houses. They should be adequate for our needs, although Abigail McKenna has been complaining, as usual. I wonder why some women married soldiers.

We wait, as we so often do.

Chapter 30

He was horse-sore and tired. Tired clean through his lean body. The cold, cutting wind was no longer even a thought. Only the flickering lights of little Franklin, Missouri. He somehow had endured the deep snow and freezing cold. The winter of 1821 had been a brutal one in the Sangre de Cristo mountains.

Finally. January 22, 1822. What had it been now? Sixty days since he had left Santa Fe.

"Well, lads, will ya have a look," said the big flush-faced Irishman, turning from the bar at the creak of the door, "our Billyboy has retarned to us. Sure, and I thought the devil might ha' been too fast for him this time."

William Becknell stood very still, his hand on the hilt of his Bowie knife. His eyes rested on Daniel Killington.

"Ya look like an old cow pattie, ya do. And ya smell like one too," Killington said.

Becknell lunged forward, grabbing the big man in a bear hug. His face cracked into a smile and he laughed a deep, hoarse laugh. "Killington, you old Irish bastard," he said pounding the man on the back. "It's good to see even the likes of you. I've not had much company these past two months. Except a few Comanche braves who didn't seem all that friendly. You're not much to be sure. But some."

Killington growled and pounded Becknell on the back in his turn. They danced a slow circle in front of the bar.

"Let me buy you a drink," Becknell said, breaking free. He tossed a rough rawhide bag with a thump onto the bar. Silver coins spilled out.

"Ya have a way about ya, that's true," said Killington, eyeing the coins. "Well, will ya look at that," he said, shaking his head. "And where might you have come upon sich riches? Did ya rob a bank or two?"

"Mighty damn close," Becknell responded, "if Santa Fe is a bank. I've never seen such money. Every kind of goods will sell there, I tell you. It's a silver mine, just sitting there above the ground. I'm going back as soon as I can get a store of goods and some wagons. I'm going to make myself a fortune. Come along, Killington."

"Lad, ya have gone daft. Goin' by horse is hard enough. No one can get through them plains in wagons. An Indian'll have your scalp hangin' from his belt befure you've made a hundred miles. And how will ya get through the mountains? Yuv lost what little sense ya ever had. No, I think I'll stay right here. But I will take that drink ya so kindly spoke of."

Daniel Killington just was dead wrong. Times were hard in Missouri in 1822. People were not about to stay put. The town, and indeed the whole state, caught the fever and the Santa Fe trade was off and running like, well, a silver rush.

The Santa Fe Trail ran for 1,200 miles over a rutted, dusty wagon track, when there was any track at all. Horses and oxen died by the score. Rain and mud bogged the heavy wagons down to their hubs or washed them away in gullies. Teams of oxen had to be unyolked and reyolked to a stuck wagon. It took incredible time and effort. Unless the weather was bad. Then it took forever.

Beyond the Great Plains lay the grim, waterless desert and then the impassable Rocky Mountains.

The Trail ran through the homelands of the Pawnee, the Cheyenne, the Comanche, and the Apache. In the early days, the Indians were fairly content to let the caravans travel through their lands. They were bribed with horses and tobacco.

But then, as more game was killed off, as more of the buffalo began to disappear, and as the grass that sustained all the animals on the Great Plains grew scarce where the caravans had traveled, the tribes became increasingly hostile. Their resistance to the wagons traveling the Trail grew. Lone hunters and small parties were attacked. Settlements were raided and settlers were massacred.

The ever-growing settlements put more and more pressure on the

Army to subdue the Indians. By 1851, the Army had established and manned a series of forts along the Trail. The furthest from Missouri was Fort Union, on the edge of the desert leading to the Great Plains, 100 miles across the Sangre de Cristo mountain range from Santa Fe.

Chapter 31

He took his handkerchief out and honked into it. A cold wind was blowing out of the Northwest. Near freezing. It was not unusual this late in February.

Canby watched at the sally port as the Confederates rolled out in line of battle about two miles away on the open plains below the low adobe fort. He knew the spot well. It was a good defensive position. Their right was anchored on the Rio Grande and their left by the low hills backing into rugged terrain. He drew his blue cloak closer around his neck.

Colonel Edward Canby was regular army. West Point 1839. The commander of the Military District of New Mexico. He was forty-four, tall and straight with a hard mouth and a fleshy nose.

Canby had a lived-in face, but his dark, haunted eyes, peering from under grey brows were, by far, his most striking feature. Like most soldiers about to enter battle, they were intense. But his seemed to look beyond the next hour. His eyes were distant and they bore in their depths a profound sadness.

He chewed on his unlit cigar as he mentally figured how many troops Sibley had brought to bear on Fort Craig. Seemed around 2,500 men to his practiced eye. A brigade then. It was important information. Of course, it helped to know what he was up against. But more important, he could tell what his troops would be up against. Even experienced officers vastly overestimated the strength of the enemy when joined in battle. And he had to know how to commit his resources.

Just a year ago he was going to resign. There was no opportunity in the Army. Maybe work in California for the railroad company. He and Louisa had liked it there. The company had seemed interested. And Louisa was tired of the desert. Being apart so much. The

Apaches had been giving the Army hell. Running them ragged.

Now this war. He had mixed emotions. This is what he had been trained for. This is where an army officer could be noticed and promoted. But killing other Americans?

He wondered how Louisa was doing in Santa Fe. If she was well. At least, she was safe with all the other officers' wives. She had wanted to be with him, but Fort Craig was too crowded and too dangerous now.

He'd been waiting for Sibley longer than he'd expected, based on the intelligence he'd been receiving. His old friend had been moving slowly. What did that mean? Winter wasn't usually considered a good time to campaign, even out here in New Mexico. And why now?

Canby sneezed. He hated getting a winter cold. His cigar was starting to taste funny.

He turned to the young cavalry officer standing beside him. The wind rumpled the officer's curly black hair. "Captain Howland, may I suggest you take your company and keep an eye on our friends out there." He gestured with his unlit cigar towards the Confederate line. "Under no circumstances do I want you to engage them."

He noticed Howland's mouth tighten. Canby spoke emphatically. "Under no circumstances. Do you understand me?"

"Not even in self-defense, sir?"

"You are not to get that close, Captain Howland. I do not want to be drawn into a battle in the open field."

"Yes, sir." Howland saluted and retreated to his small command.

"I don't like 'em seeing us back down from a fight. It'll make 'em more aggressive." Canby turned his head towards the short, wiry man on his left. He was older. His face showed his age, more like leather than skin. The man spat tobacco juice into the dirt at his feet.

"Colonel Carson, I have no intention of engaging General Sibley on ground of his choosing." The man he was talking to was Kit Carson who commanded the First Regiment of New Mexico Volunteers.

Carson was in his early fifties, with even, attractive features. A deep chested man of medium height. It was unusual to see a clean-shaven man in the Territories. A nice face until you looked into his blue eyes. He had the soulless eyes of a killer.

"We got enough men," Carson said. "More than they got."

Canby brushed at a spot of dirt on his uniform sleeve before returning his gaze to Carson. He didn't like having his decisions questioned.

And not by a volunteer colonel, no matter how well known. But he needed Carson and his New Mexico volunteers. He distrusted them, but they were all he had. He gazed out in order to collect himself. He kept his voice level, keeping the anger out of it.

"That may be, but I believe it would be foolhardy with so few regulars among us." Canby stopped and turned to look again at the smaller man.

"And I question whether we have more men than they do, Colonel Carson. Moreover, the Rebels have a strong defensive position. Your men are untrained and I believe are incapable of maneuvering under fire."

Carson frowned again and started to speak, but Canby talked over him. "I intend to remain in this posture and allow General Sibley to attack us if he so desires." Just because Carson was famous didn't mean he knew how to fight an organized enemy.

"I don't like it."

"So be it, Colonel Carson. I'm in command here. It is my ..." His words were drowned out by the thunder of hooves as Howland's cavalry left the fort through the sally port. Carson had turned on his heel. Canby never got to finish his sentence.

A line of Confederate infantry from the left of the Confederate position advanced towards the fort. Canby opened on them with artillery as they approached. Too high. But they retreated anyway. A feint then. Meant to draw him out.

Chapter 32

Kit Carson was a legend even then. Born on Christmas Eve in 1809, he had become a bright strand in the woof and weave of Western history. His exploits were the stuff of young boy's dreams.

Carson's family moved to Boone's Lick, Missouri, when he was an infant and farmed land owned by Daniel Boone's sons. The Boone and the Carson families became friends and the families intermarried. Adaline Carson, Daniel Boone's great grand-niece, was one of little Kit's playmates.

But the frontier was a bitter life and farming was a dangerous business. Carson's father died in a farming accident when he was a child. His penniless mother remarried.

Kit did not get on well with his stepfather. And his stepfather apprenticed him to a saddle-maker in Franklin, Missouri, the town at the head of the Santa Fe Trail that had been opened by Jim Becknell the year before, in 1822.

Business didn't suit this young free spirit and he slipped away from his employer to become a mountain man in Santa Fe. Carson was sixteen. He became known among those rough men as a reliable companion and a good fighter. Grizzly Bears and Indians were the enemy. It was a rugged existence fraught with risk. It nurtured hard men.

Like so many events in life, an accidental meeting nudged Carson onto a new path and into fame. In 1841, he was returning from his home in Missouri where he had just placed his daughter in school. He met a young Army officer named John C. Fremont on a steamboat on the Missouri River. Fremont had been tasked by the Army to survey the Oregon Trail. He hired Carson as a guide. Carson got $100, the most money he had ever made.

There followed three expeditions and in 1846 both Fremont and

Carson participated in the Bear Flag revolt, a rebellion to free California from Mexico. Fremont had worked hard, perhaps under President James Polk's prodding, to ignite that fight. Polk was known to want both Texas and California for the Union.

Carson's fame was spreading through government reports, newspaper articles and a set of dime novels that exaggerated and romanticized his exploits. He liked that.

Following his service in the Mexican-American War of 1846, which forced Mexico to recognize the Rio Grande as the border of Texas and ceded much of the West to the United States, Carson sought to be and was appointed an Indian Agent. Then, finally, came the Civil War. Carson liked to fight.

In 1861, he enlisted in the Union Army. Brevetted a Lt. Colonel of the New Mexico Volunteers, reflecting his fame and popularity, he was ordered to Fort Craig under the command of Colonel Edward Canby.

Chapter 33

Colonel Tom Green, of the Confederate States of America, didn't like assuming command of the army. It wasn't right. General Sibley should be here leading his men, not him.

An aide to Sibley had brought the order for him to take command. Sibley was sick again. Whatever sick was. But why, when this could be a decisive battle. They could win the New Mexico Territory for the Confederacy right here. Most of the Union Army was in front of them.

Green knew he would have struggled off his own deathbed to lead his Texans. Green was a tall man with a hard, chiseled face. His cheeks were stubbled. But the striking feature were his eyes. They seemed to see through a man.

Green choreographed several hours of maneuvering in front of the fort. He drew out skirmishers. Some cavalry. Minor elements. As darkness gathered, Green realized Canby would not take the bait. In his judgment, the fort was too well fortified to attack in a frontal assault. His field howitzers were useless against its thick adobe walls. He summoned his aides.

"Each regiment is to withdraw in good order. The 4th is to act as rear guard. Order the artillery to remain in place until the 4th is ready to withdraw. They will withdraw with the 4th as their guard." His aides scattered.

The withdrawal began, with the Rebels shouting curses and gibes back towards the fort. Canby couldn't hear, but he could see and there was no mistaking the gestures. He gritted his teeth and sent out additional cavalry to keep an eye on the Confederate movements. As he watched, a shaggy, unkempt man came up beside him. He had a stout strong body on stubby legs. And he smelled really bad, a notable feat in the open air, among a hoard of unwashed men. Canby took another step sideways.

"Begging your pardon, sir, but I have an idea how we can make those secesh boys right miserable. The Spy Company would like to do it, sir."

"What did you have in mind, Captain Graydon?" Paddy Graydon had formed a company of loyalists in Tucson, Arizona. He was their natural leader, being the bartender in town. They had been driven out of Tucson by the secessionists. The war was personal to them.

"Well now, I'll tell you, sir."

Campfires burned bright in the Confederate camp. Pickets had been set out and the soldiers for once had enough food. Foragers had found some stores. No one was expecting any fighting, not from the yellow-bellies. Certainly not a raid.

Graydon and four of his men moved through the night leading two old mules. Graydon whispered, "Be quiet as a little mouse, you boys. And be careful with them mules or we're all liable to meet the good Lord before our time."

The two mules each labored under a heavy box packed with a half dozen 24-pound howitzer shells. The men proceeded slowly, picking their way through the darkness. Clouds covered the moon except in brief intervals. In those intervals, they went to the ground and waited. The noise and the light of campfires were their guide.

Graydon raised his hand. "Did you hear something?" he whispered.

The man beside him nodded. There was movement about 150 yards away, on their right. They could make out the silhouette of a man. A picket. They'd reached the Confederate camp.

Graydon motioned for them to move to their left. They moved a few hundred yards behind a low hill. They shed their packs and drew the mules up. One of the soldiers struck a match which he shielded with his hand. Another did the same. At a nod from Graydon they lit the slow fuses to each box and gave the mules a swat towards the Confederate camp. The mules took off. Graydon smiled and grabbed his pack.

"Let's be on our way, lads. Best we put as much distance between us and them as we may."

They had gone about three hundred yards when one of his men let out a shout. Graydon turned on him with his fist raised. Which is where it stayed.

Along behind them lumbered the two mules, following the leader. The men broke into a run.

The explosions brought the Confederate camp to arms. All five Yankees survived the furor by the dint of strong legs and good wind. The mules did not.

Graydon wondered all the way back to the fort how he was going to explain this to Colonel Canby without becoming the laughing-stock of the post. He shook his head. Maybe he couldn't. Maybe he'd just tell a little fib. Yep, that's what he'd do. No harm to be done there.

Chapter 34

February 21, 1862 was clear and bitter cold. Still dark. The stars were like points of ice. Even the dog who had huddled up against Ezra Davis was shivering. Snow dusted its fur. No tents. They'd had to leave a lot of wagons back at the river to come along another way.

Ezra Davis pulled the thin blanket tighter around his body. His stomach gripped him. They'd been on half rations for twenty days now, with the exception of the night before last.

Country up here in New Mexico weren't worth nothin', Ezra thought. Not to grow stuff. Couldn't say why Sibley and old President Davis wanted it. Made no sense.

It was a dry camp. There had been no water since his canteen ran out eight hours ago. His mouth was parched. It would be dawn soon. It had been six months since he had signed up in Austin and he still hadn't seen a good fight.

Sibley had taken the Army of New Mexico, his name for the Texas Mounted Volunteers, inland from the Rio Grande, north through the mountains, so Canby wouldn't know what they were up to. That is, he had ordered it. Colonel Tom Green was in charge. The demonstration in front of Fort Craig hadn't brought the Union Army out to fight and they were now in a pickle.

At least that's what Ezra was thinking. He sure didn't like leaving 3,000 Union troops between them and home. Even if they were yellow-bellies. Davis scratched at his side.

The body lice were a misery. Nothing seemed to help. But the boys sure made the best of it. You had to say that.

The lice races were popular. Boys would heat up a piece of tin over the fire until it was tolerably hot and each would put a louse in the middle. They would be rooting and punching at each other, betting even, to see whose louse got itself off the fastest.

Ezra was still half asleep, thinking about Becky.

Sure did surprise me for a girl I been sorta courtin', he thought. When I told her I'd gone and volunteered, I reckoned she'd be weepin' and carryin' on to beat the band.

Nope, she preened up and said how proud she was of me. How 'twerent right, them Yankees fightin' us 'cause we wanted to go on our own. Said her grandpappy had fought in the Mexican War just so Texas could go its own way.

"I wonder, does she have her eye on some other fella?" he muttered aloud. "Ain't had no letter from her. Writ her three times now."

A boot nudged him, roughlike in his ribs. It was attached to the First Sergeant of Company D, Second Regiment.

"Get your ass moving, Davis. Get them boys up too. Ain't got all day. Eat yur breakfast, what there is of it. Pyron and us been ordered to move out with Scurry."

Ezra sat up, the blanket wrapped around his shoulders. He'd been on guard duty, it seemed half the night. The dog went with him to keep him awake. Good thing, as Captain Willis was always checking up on him. Didn't think he was soldier enough. Davis kicked out at the man sleeping a foot or two away.

"Walter, now don't you pretend you ain't heard that. We gotta get us a fire going. What we got? Dry beef? At least some biscuit left. You got any water?"

Walter was maybe eighteen now, Ezra couldn't right remember. Wouldn't stay at home like he shoulda. No damn sense. Thought this was some kinda adventure, mouthin' off about how we wasn't gonna let any Yankees tell us what to do. Ma shouldn'ta let him come, but Walter's headstrong.

Walter lifted an eyelid and yawned. "Darn cold." He jumped up and rolled his blanket.

"You got any water?" Ezra repeated.

Walter shook his head. "Ain't had none since yesterday."

"Dang," Ezra grumbled as he scratched at the lice again. "No coffee. Can't ride without no coffee."

Walter laughed. "You getting just like that old dog, Ezra. You got fleas."

They'd picked up the dog in Mesilla, or rather it had picked them up. They called him Twitchal.

Kinda nice having him around. Sorta like home. Hain't been no trouble. Sometimes get one of the wagons to carry him. Mostly he would trot along behind their horses. Dart into the brush every once in a while, chasin' something. 'Twerent the only dog in the Company, but Twitchal were the best hunter. Looked like he'd been eating better than them.

Had hell to pay in camp last night. Big fella, name of Ben Slater. Well, the boys somehow got the notion he wouldn't fight. So no one would let him mess at their campfire. Had one all by hisself like. Anyway, last night Jake Kinerd's horse got loose and ate up all Slater's rations. We'd just pulled 'em, being as little as they was. Slater got the notion the horse were mine, don't know how, and he come for me.

Shouted at me, so, naturally, I called him a liar. He didn't take that none too well. Musta been a clap of thunder like. I seen about forty million stars on my way back head over my heels.

Did my damnedest to get up but his fist kept getting in the way. Good thing Lieutenant Wright come along when he did. I'd sure have beat up Slater real bad.

So I weren't movin' any too good as well as being froze near through. My horse jostling along and me with no coffee. Walter skittered up beside me.

"You know where we goin'?" Walter asked.

"Head back to the river, upstream of the fort. A ford where we can cross back over. Fellow tol' me it was name of Valverde."

Pryon and his boys up ahead. Two hundred of us strung out 'bout half a mile on the narrow trail. Me with my blanket wrapped around me to keep a little warm. Damn Sibley, he didn't tell us it were a winter campaign. Most of the boys had less on than me. Well, all that bein' said, I just weren't in the best of moods.

The unmistakable pop of musketry snapped his musing.

"Pyron's at it!" someone shouted.

"By God, are we gonna let Pyron whip 'em afore we gets in our licks?" Walter said, all exited like, taking his double-barreled shotgun out of its sling.

Horses spurred to a gallop towards the gunfire, everyone a yellin' loud and high.

Chapter 35

Canby had easily seen through the Confederate feint in front of the fort. The stub of an chewed cigar stained the corner of his desk. His patrols had detected most of the Confederate forces crossing the river below the fort.

The sneeze took him by surprise. It snapped his head forward. He grabbed at his handkerchief and brought it to his mouth in time to catch a second sneeze. He rubbed at his nose. Now it was getting red and irritated. No matter. He retreated into his thoughts.

It was obvious to him that the Texans intended to bypass Fort Craig and leave him on their supply line. That was strange. Nothing he would have done. But what was their plan? Did they intend to double back and attack him from the other side? Or attempt to surround him and starve him out?

Canby sat at his desk, gazing at the bare adobe walls of his office. To his left a lantern flicked, barely reducing the gloom in the low, cramped room.

"They have to be headed north," he muttered. "They'll probably cross back over the river at the Valverde ford, six miles up. It's the only ford that a lot of men can use."

It was good ground to pick a fight if he could get there first. A key strategic point. Canby did not want it in Sibley's hands. He really didn't see that he had a choice.

He raised his head. "Lieutenant." His aide appeared through the door and came to attention. "Sir," he said, saluting. Canby sneezed again. He waved his handkerchief in the lieutenant's direction.

"Please find Colonel Roberts and tell him I'd like a word with him immediately." His nose was getting stuffed up and the words were muted.

Ten minutes later, there was a knock on the open door. Lt. Colonel Benjamin Roberts was a man of medium height. At nearly fifty, his dark hair was already thinning and gray in places. Canby thought he was a good soldier. A West Point graduate, even if he had quit the Army.

"Colonel Roberts, I believe the enemy intends to cross the river at Valverde. We cannot let that happen. You must get there first and hold the ford."

––––––––––

Robert's cavalry units, under the command of Thomas Duncan, surmounted a string of rising hills. Major Duncan, a heavy man in his late thirties, urged on the four companies of cavalry that Roberts had ordered ahead to reach Valverde before the Confederates could invest it. He saw the river was just a mile ahead.

The air was clear and cold. There was a wind blowing towards him across the river, ruffling his long side burns. Duncan didn't see movement. He motioned his men into a gallop.

The horses splashed across the river at the lower ford. They dismounted at Duncan's order, grasping carbines, and spreading out in the bosque on the right side of the ford, the river at their back. Duncan walked the line. Almost three hundred men. Now came the hard part. Waiting.

"Settle down." Duncan's voice was almost gentle. It betrayed none of the anxiety he felt. "We need to hold this ground. Our artillery and reinforcements will be here soon. Don't shoot unless I give the order." Some men bit their lips or nodded. A few muttered.

"Major," a soldier said loudly. Duncan whirled towards him. "I see somethin' stirrin' in that grove of cottonwoods yonder." Duncan moved down the line to the man and stared in the direction the man was pointing. He was uncertain, but something did seem to be moving.

He motioned over an officer. "Lieutenant Chaflin, take a company and see what's going on over there." He pointed to the location of the movement about a half mile off among the cottonwood trees. "Approach cautiously and watch yourself."

The terrain was overgrown and wooded. It took ten minutes for Chaflin to reach the cottonwood grove. A surprised Confederate scout snapped off a shot to alert the troops behind and retreated deeper into the grove. The Confederate main body moved rapidly forward and opened a ragged fire on Chaflin and his men.

Chaflin, sensing a large body of the enemy, and with less than seventy men of his own, turned tail and scrambled back towards Duncan's lines. Pyron, followed by his Texans, broke out of the woods in hot pursuit.

Chaflin was riding at full gallop and shouting as he came into view of the Union line, but Duncan couldn't make out the words. He did seem to be in a lather.

Then Pyron burst into view of Duncan's dismounted command. Duncan opened fire.

A bullet holed Pryon's billowing coat. He reined in so abruptly that his horse skidded on loose dirt and almost fell. He had to fight for control. His men almost ran him down.

"Dismount," Pryon yelled. "Spread out and seek cover," he shouted, sweeping his hat off as he turned.

"Hold your positions, men," Duncan ordered his Union soldiers, calmly walking his line. "We seem to be outnumbered. We have to hold the ford until help comes. Make every shot count."

Pyron leaped off his horse. "I want a line of battle there." He pointed back and forth along an old arroyo cutting across the river valley. It appeared to be the old channel for the river about 400 yards from the Union lines. He motioned forward a captain who was still mounted. Bullets snapped at tree branches near their heads. Falling branches brushed their arms. Pryon ignored them. The officer leaned from his horse towards Pryon.

"Captain, advise Colonel Scurry immediately that I have confronted a large Union force and we are engaged. They are between us and the river. I estimate the Union forces to be well in excess of our number. We need reinforcements at the earliest possible moment.

Chapter 36

Medical Notes of Dr. Edward N. Convey
(Medical Director of the Confederate Army of New Mexico)
February 17, 1862

I was called in today to treat General Henry Sibley, Commanding General. The patient has been subject to repeated bouts of illness during the course of the last month and I have kept him under close observation. He presents with acute stomach pains, accompanied by vomiting and nausea.

After examining him, I have determined that he suffers from colic. The acute abdominal pain may be the result of kidney stones, but it is impossible under these circumstances to reach a firm diagnosis.

His condition has been complicated by the excessive consumption of alcohol which has been an ongoing issue. The drinking may be in response to the pain he is experiencing.

He is entirely too unwell for service. I have strongly advised him to turn over the command of this army to Colonel Green until he has recovered sufficiently to resume command.

Chapter 37

We busted out at a gallop, a yellin' to beat all. Walter was leading the pack, waving his arm for us to hurry on. He turned back towards me. His long dark hair whipped into his face.

"Dang, Ezra," he shouted at me, the wind carrying his voice, "we gonna get us some Yankees." I weren't in quite such a hurry as Walter. Never was. Hesper, he was some place even further back.

Looked like smoke was comin' outa our mouths, it was so cold. Must ha' been a sight to see, us galloping up.

Major Pyron put an end to all that. Waving' his hat and shouting. Wanted us down off our horses and inta an old slough to the left of the other boys who was there already. Our first sergeant hurried us along a little rough for my taste.

"Now, Reed," I tol' him, "you be a little more c'siderate or I'm gonna see to you myself." Didn't have no effect on Reed, he just went and pushed at Walter.

There was lots of cottonwood about. Groves scattered along the valley, must have been a coupla miles wide, where the river broadened out, shallow and easy to cross. The ground was sloping down, with sand ridges and small hills runnin' in lines along the river.

A cold wind was blowin'. Made it right uncomfortable. Wondered where Twitchal had made off to. Dog knew when there was trouble coming. Made hisself scarce. Smart dog.

Walter was hunkered down right beside me. He started to stand up. I grabbed at his arm.

"You got any brains? Them Yankees'll use you for target practice. They got them long-range rifles. You got to be cautious like."

"Ah, Ezra, I jest wanted to see me a live Yankee afore we kill 'em all." Boy never had no sense.

I stuck my head up a little beside a rock so only one eye was stuck out. I could see the Yankees 'tween us and the river. Seemed to me like they was cowerin' down. I couldn't right blame 'em, we being Texas boys.

Pulled my head back in pretty quick when one of them miniballs kicked up the dirt an' dusted my face good. I was spittin' that dirt for a while.

Pyron was ridin' his horse up and down behind the arroyo, shouting for us to keep our heads down. The Yankees were ashootin' at him. Didn't blink an eye. Sat tall. Good officer Pyron, not like some.

The other regiments began a comin' along as quick as their worn-out old horses would carry 'em. Any time we heard a fight, everyone would make for the sound of the gunfire. Never waited for word. That's how it was. Sutton's 7th started filling in the arroyo along our left, extendin' our line.

Then Dirty Shirt Scurry arrives with the 4th making a hell of a lot of noise. We calls him that fer the reason we never seen him cleaned up. He got down next to Sutton's men. I can tell you I was sure glad to see 'em. Must have been 3,000 Yankees out there, maybe more. No more than about 2,000 of us.

We was spread out considerable to cover our line. And what with the Yankees 300 or 400 yards away, blastin' away at us with their cannon. Shootin' way too high and doing nothin' but wastin' powder. All except when they hit the woods near our horses. Must 'a been fifty of 'em broke loose for the river. We weren't ever gonna seem 'em again.

We was armed mostly with shotguns, which was useless at this distance. The few of us with long-range guns played on them Yankees, but I have to say it didn't do much.

Musta been close to an hour, my head pressed up under that bank. I was breathin' steam, my teeth a clickin'. I was nearly froze with cold. I couldn't feel my toes. Good thing we weren't goin' nowhere. But them Yankee boys was between us and that river so I can tell you, I was itchin' to fight. I was thirsty as hell.

Colonel Green comes thunderin' up on his big horse with maybe two or three companies more. I got no idea where our General was, though rumor had it he was tucked in bed with his bottle. So, Green was our man.

I saw him and Major Pyron talking. Pyron was tellin' him how the Yankees was set up. I could see him gesturing. Green was listenin' pretty close. Cannon ball hit about six feet away from them and bounced. Broke up their little party darn quick. Then Green done rode off.

Must have been another half hour, us keeping pretty close to the ground, when this cheerin' comes on our left. I looked over that way and sees Phil Fulcrod comin' up with our own artillery. About nine o'clock, judgin' by the sun. Formed right up in front of our line, unlimbered and started giving them Yankees hell.

Made hisself a target though. Cannon ball gutted one of his horses. Some blood got on my face. I wiped at it.

Fulcrod's men started to go down. One, name of Ewell Martin, fell down into the arroyo by Walter and me, holding his gut with both his hands. Knew him from back home. Blood was runnin' out 'tween his fingers. He was cryin'. Tried to stop the bleedin' but there was nothin' we could do. Then he jest stopped movin'.

Walter, he stared. Never seen a man die before. I ain't never seen one die like that.

There weren't enough men to work the guns no more. Fulcrod was workin' the guns with his own hands. Several of the boys, includin' Hesper, jumped up out of the slough to help. They started doin' what they could, Fulcrod a shoutin' them instructions. Walter made as if to get up but I stood on him. No sense in takin' unnecessary risks, there bein' so many boys out with the guns already.

Then Teel come into the line with the balance of the artillery, but all his horses was killed quick. Had to move and work 'em by hand, but we made do. Our artillery must have been outnumbered 'bout three to one but we did our work on the Yankees.

Finally Major Raquet with a portion of the 4th came into line on our right and our full force was in action. Then the fun sure started.

Chapter 38

He spurred his horse to the top of the hill. Colonel Benjamin Roberts reined in overlooking the Rio Grande. It had been a difficult ride. He was overweight and sweating in spite of the cold.

The boil on his inner thigh had burst and the constant motion had irritated it, causing him a lot of pain. He gritted his teeth as the horse strained up the rise and muttered under his breath. He was almost fifty. Why, in heaven's name, had he volunteered? He should have listened to Sarah.

The sun was high in the sky but it didn't give off any heat. There was a light cold wind in his face off the river. The wind ruffled his cloak. He really wanted to smoke his pipe, but he didn't want to do so in front of the men.

He looked back over his shoulder. The infantry was just behind. Another fifteen or twenty minutes for the Union artillery to come up. As he waited, he took in the battlefield. It was like watching a tableau from a perfect seat in the theater. The sound of the muskets was faint, but sharp and clear. He could see the puffs of black powder smoke caught by the breeze and snatched away.

Major Duncan's 300 men had their back to the river. Roberts was attracted to a movement on his right among the slanted shadows of a group of cottonwoods. He focused. Groups of Rebel soldiers were moving. The Confederates were extending their line to his right to attempt to anchor on the river below Duncan and envelope Duncan's position.

Roberts turned and motioned for Lieutenant Charles Meinhold to come close. He pointed out the Rebel movements with a few words and sent Meinhold galloping to warn Duncan of the peril.

He could see Meinhold wade the river, water splashing around the withers of his horse. The occasional Rebel musket ball feathered the surface. Meinhold dismounted on the fly beside Duncan. Dirt flew up at his heels.

Roberts could see him talk and gesticulate emphatically to his right. Duncan turned and shouted something. About fifty skirmishers left the Federal line and entered the heavy woods at a run. Roberts view was obscured by powder smoke that seemed to fill the woods where it was sheltered from the wind, but he could hear a flurry of musket fire.

The infantry was coming up. The captain of the Fifth Cavalry rode up and saluted Roberts.

"Where do you want us, sir?"

Roberts pointed to the upper part of Duncan's line. "Get across and deploy your men as skirmishers to the left. We need to hold them until we can get more reinforcements."

To Roberts the tableaux below moved in slow motion. He could do nothing more. Canby had to send more troops. He had already dispatched a rider. The entire Confederate army seemed to be massing. He didn't have enough men.

The sound of approaching hooves attracted his attention. Captain Alexander McRae breasted the hill with his six 6-pounder guns. McRae was a dark-haired slender man, with a mustache and feathery goatee. He was regular Army. They said he was brave.

Roberts hand described to McRae a position on the west side of the river about 400 yards from the Confederate lines and opposite the Confederate artillery. "I want your cannons there," Roberts ordered. "With all haste, please."

McRae and his company skittered down the hill, leaving a trail of dust in their wake. Colonel Roberts was becoming frustrated. He could see the Confederate reinforcements coming into play along the north side of the field.

He turned to Lt. Meinhold who was by his side again. "I need to get our artillery to the east bank where they can engage the Rebels who are coming in. That wooded area is critical." He gestured to the area Duncan had contested earlier. "Go to Major Duncan and tell him he must give us cover urgently. We will need fifteen minutes to get Captain McRae's men across." Meinhold clattered away to cross the cold river again.

To Roberts's annoyance nothing happened. Duncan couldn't seem to suppress the Rebel's fire. His artillery was stranded on the west side of the Rio Grande and the Confederates were reinforcing their positions almost at will.

McRae forged into the river in the face of a brisk fire. One of his men screamed and fell. One of the guns hung up on a knot of rock. "Hitch another horse to that gun. Pull it out. Let's do it smartly."

Finally, he was across. "Get the guns unlimbered," he called. "I want them here and here and here. Picket the horses over there." He pointed to a spot perhaps twenty yards in the rear. "We'll be moving up soon enough. Load canister. Make sure you elevate over our lines."

They were sitting in an exposed position, but there was no return fire yet. McRae's regulars started to pepper the slough beyond the Union lines with canister. The bursting canister sent a swarm of deadly musket balls snipping at the undergrowth and snapping at the branches of the cottonwoods.

They were pretty much firing blind. McRae waved the smoke away from his face so he could see the point of impact. McRae saw no discernible effect from his first volley, but he urged the men to keep up the rate of fire. For once, he had enough powder and shell.

Excitement played on McRae's face. This was his first action against a real army. He hadn't had much experience against the Indians. They were too mobile. The cavalry didn't take field artillery.

He touched the arm of one of his men. "There's movement over there in the slough." It could have been the wind. The men pushed at the heavy gun until it pointed towards the area of the movement.

McRae wiped the sweat away from his eyes. The guns were hot to be near, even in the cold wind. And they were shatteringly loud, even through the pieces of rag he had stuffed into his ears. His ears were ringing. Lately he felt as if he didn't hear so well.

Muttering curses at Duncan, Roberts dispatched another messenger to Canby at Fort Craig. The main Confederate forces would reach the Valverde ford by noon and he would be overwhelmed unless reinforced. He hadn't been bothered by his boil for hours.

Chapter 39

Well, Teel, he done limbered up his two guns and moved off to the left. Guess it were too hot for him to stay. I sure felt that way, what with mini balls nippin' the dirt above my head. And me layin' there froze solid.

It were snowing in small flurries, us out in the open. Why wasn't them lice froze solid too, I ask you? I can tell you for a certainty mine wasn't. I was scratchin' to beat all.

Waitin' was getting at me. There weren't nothing to do but keep down. Our shotguns couldn't reach the Union boys so we just hid. Walter, bein' a kid, was nervous. Always wantin' to talk. Excited like. Couldn't hardly hush him up.

I was nawin' on a hunk of salt pork I had in my pack. Felt like it was nawin' back at me. I still didn't have no water but I was hungry enough to eat a horse. Hadn't come to that yet though. Figured how it would.

Walter was smoking his clay pipe. The artillery fire seemed to let up on us. I could hear it more off to my right. When I got a peek, I seen lots of Union boys movin' up the river.

"Looks like we got trouble comin'," I said to Walter, pointin' over that way.

Musta been about one o'clock judging by how light it was. It were then Colonel Green came stormin' back with a slew more men and a couple more guns and got set up on our right maybe half a mile from us.

Good thing too 'cause all hell done broke loose. A bunch of boys near to us pulled back and mounted up. They moved off to the right, on down the line.

There were a lot of musket fire up there and judging by the sounds, their horses musta got shot up pretty bad. Maybe men too. Couldn't see, there being a sand bank in the way.

They was bein' attacked pretty hard, but seemed to be holding on. Can't say I was sorry to be where I was. I ain't a coward, but I can manage to wait my turn.

Now I seen Yankee artillery movin' up the river. They was gonna cross too. I soon heard guns start to fire again. Their guns. They sound different from ours. Closer now. Looked like we was being hard – pressed on our right.

"Move right, move right. Fill in the line." That was Reed, the first sergeant. I tucked up and crawled right a few hundred yards, behind Walter. Walter still had that pipe stuck in his mouth.

Not as cozy here as down under the sandbank. More exposed like. I hunkered down.

But I could see what was happenin', and it were amazin'. See, we got this company of cavalry. Old Sibley couldn't get 'em proper weapons, so he equips 'em with these eight-feet lances tipped in iron.

I don't know much 'bout war, just bein' a Texas boy, but I shor wouldn't want to try to prick a Union boy holdin' a rifle with a toothpick like that. No matter. Were lots of boys likin' the glitter and polish. They did look mighty pretty.

I hear this bugle and Captain Lang over on the right, he signals his company of lancers forward. It's maybe three, four hundred yards to the Union lines. They moved out from behind the embankment and spread out into a line. First they trot and then they break into a gallop, lowering them long poles.

Nothing happenin' on the Union side. It's beautiful. Cold even light. Never seen nothin' like it, horses stretchin' out and men leaning into them, holdin' them long sticks. Walter was babblin' beside me. How we was going to bust the Yankee line.

Dust a comin' up behind them from the sandy spots. At about 100 yards, I see movement over on the Yankee side. Then the whole damn line is covered with powder smoke. Then a second time.

If you ain't ever heard a horse been shot, well I tell ya, it's a terrible sound. Musta been forty horses down, strugglin' to get up. Men spilled all over. Some moanin'. Some not moving at all.

What's left of the boys start turning to the left. Across the Yankee line as they try to escape. I see more of them getting picked off.

More horses falling. I seen one fall onto an officer and kick at him as it tried to get back up. His face was a bloody mess. Couldn't see him move none.

Walter, lookin' on, had his mouth open. His clay pipe had dropped out to the ground. Weren't talkin' for once. But he were holdin' his head down. Can't say that for Hesper Evans a few yards away. Hesper signed up with us.

He nearly died of the yellow fever inoculation we got at Fort Bliss. Was sick for close on a week. He didn't die though.

Didn't teach him no sense. Never had any to start with. Died now, you betcha. Bullet threw him back maybe five feet. Weren't much left of his left arm. Damn fool. I liked old Hesper. Made it harder.

Walter bent over gaggin' at the sight an' moved towards him. I put my hand on his arm.

"Don't. He's dead." I just knew.

Walter was breathin' short and hard. Woulda puked if his throat weren't so dry, I bet. I tol' him to get used to it. It were an adventure. Just like old Hesper said.

Maybe Walter were growing up a little. I scratched my itch and held my shotgun close. I was still damn thirsty. Liken to perish.

No sooner had I settled down than our Lieutenant come a bustlin' down the line. Young fellow, maybe twenty-two. Didn't know if he shaved. Not often, I reckon.

"I want every third man to fall back and form up over behind there." He gestured to a hill a couple of hundred yards back, a little on our left. "Rest of you stay in place." I could see the same thing happening all down the center of our line.

"Stay low, ya'll." His voice was a growl. "Don't let the Yankees see you. Come on now. Move out."

I looked over at Walter next to me and motioned for him to come on as soon as the Lieutenant turned his back. I didn't want to go without Walter. Wherever we was going.

Chapter 40

He was tired and cold. It had been a long day already. It was past two o'clock. They had been fighting since noon. Why was he so tired?

Colonel Benjamin Roberts was trying to concentrate. The boil on his thigh was hurting again, distracting him. God, am I too old to be in command? he thought. Should I have stayed in Iowa, tucked safely away in my law practice?

Sarah was sure riled. She didn't like his returning to the Army. His lips broke into a small smile of recollection. She wouldn't even come out to Santa Fe with the other wives. Nope. She made a point of staying at home. Said a piece too.

Why had he come? That was harder. Boredom, sure. Some of that. He hadn't missed the Army. Well, maybe in some ways.

It wasn't the Negros. He didn't like slavery, but they weren't worth dying for. He shook his head at the idea. His horse stirred, sending a sharp pain up his thigh.

No, it was his country. He had a deep belief in his country. Even if that fool Lincoln was president. He shrugged off his doubts with a physical motion.

He was watching from his vantage point on the hill as the left steadily advanced against the Confederate right. The men moved in a long line, slowly from tree to tree. Sporadically. Moving and stopping to fire. Then staying still behind a tree to reload. Puffs of black smoke rising to obscure his view, then swirling away in the breeze. His boys driving back the Rebel skirmishers.

He glanced up at the sky to try to judge the weather. The clouds looked like dark, woolly sheep, rushing to flock together. It would snow soon. It was cold enough. What effect would that have on the battle? he wondered. The men would be cold. But it was better than rain. Rain would wet the gunpowder and make the guns less reliable. So best it should snow.

An absurd feeling of pleasure suffused him, looking at the clouds. His mouth relaxed, oblivious for the moment of men dying in the field below.

"Excuse me, sir," his aide said moving to his side, snapping him out of his musing, "I think you should see this." He was pointing to the left in the shallow valley below.

"What the hell?" Roberts couldn't believe what he saw. A company of mounted lancers challenging his men. His men with rifles. It was like a dream from 200 years ago. It would be a massacre. Foolishness.

Down below, Captain Theodore Dodd of the Colorado Volunteers watched the Confederate cavalry. He'd seen a cavalry attack before. His boys had practiced for it.

"Form the line." He shouted at his company to be heard over the din of battle. "Three deep. Remember how we did it. First row kneeling. Second standing. Each row fires in volley at my command. Pass back your rifles. Third row reloads. Come on now, hurry. Good. Good."

The cavalry went from a trot into a gallop with their lances raised.

Dodd couldn't believe his eyes. Lances?

Two hundred yards. A hundred-fifty. Fifty yards. "Fire," he shouted.

The first Union volley caught the Texans. As the gun smoke blew away in the breeze, Roberts could see men and horses lashed in blood strewn across the Union left.

Who were the Confederates charging? Roberts wondered. Ted Dodd, he recalled. The Colorado Volunteers. Hard men. Not like the New Mexicans.

Unbelievably, the Texans kept coming. A hundred yards. Fifty. Forty yards from Dodd's men. "Fire, fire, damn it," Roberts shouted although no one could hear him. Suddenly the air burst with the report of the Union muskets and horses and men collapsed into a bloody mass.

"Thank God," Roberts exclaimed. The remnants of the Confederate company of lancers were turning away from the hail of bullets and crossing parallel to the center of the Union line.

McRae was across the river with his battery of guns, but he hadn't had time to unlimber yet. Colonel Carson and his New Mexico volunteers were coming into the center of the Union line and starting to fire on the horsemen. More horses fell. The sounds of screaming horses reached Roberts. It was a sound he had never grown accustomed to. Strangely, it affected him more than the screams of wounded men. Although, God knows, he felt for those boys.

Dodd looked over his men. "You boys did good." That was true, but this was their first action. Maybe he should give them a few seconds to regroup before moving forward again. "Fall back to the embankment," he ordered.

Roberts could see the advance against the Confederate right stall, falling back to regroup. He contemplated the battlefield. He turned to his aide to tell Todd to resume his advance. They needed to maintain pressure on the Confederates.

His attention was caught by cheering behind him. He turned in time to see Colonel Canby ride into view with 600 hundred reinforcements and two more cannons.

Canby rode directly to Roberts and saluted. "Colonel Roberts. I assume command. I will cross the river and review the situation on the ground. We seem to be in a lull. Please co-ordinate the removal of the wounded. I've brought ammunition. See that it is distributed to our troops."

"Yes, sir," Roberts said, returning the salute, glad to be free of the responsibility.

Canby rode behind the Union line, oblivious to the occasional musket ball that whizzed past. He needed to see Duncan, who was commanding the right of his line.

"Major Duncan, I want you to advance and swing left with the right section of your line. Hall's battery will advance in support." Canby made a door closing movement with his hands. "When you have advanced sufficiently, you will be in position to enfilade the Rebels. Do you understand?"

"Yes, sir. But I will need more troops."

"I have ordered Colonel Carson to support you on the left."

"When shall I attack?"

"Immediately."

Duncan turned as Canby remounted. Duncan wasn't comfortable.

Duncan's men had advanced about 200 yards, driving in the Confederates. In another hundred yards they would be able to fire down the Confederate line. This had gone better than Duncan had anticipated. That was, until the Confederate cavalry attacked. These men had guns and swords, not lances. His men froze in place.

Major Henry W. Raquet of the Fourth Mounted Texas Volunteers yelled at his 250 men to charge. He loved the feel of his horse pounding under him and the wind on his face. He took off his hat and used it in a continuous sweeping motion to urge his men forward. They were going to take the Union cannon if it killed him.

The first Union volley hit his men when he was a hundred yards from the gun. He looked back and was horrified at the carnage. A cannon shell exploded nearby, felling more cavalry. No choice. He had to retreat or a counterattack would expose the entire line to the Union forces. He urged his horse to turn aside, shouting at his remaining cavalrymen.

"Lieutenant Hall," Duncan ordered, "limber up your gun and move forward. He raised his voice. "You men," he gestured to several companies on his left, "move forward to support the battery."

Carson's volunteers, seeing the retreating Rebels and the movement on the right, surged forward in pursuit, opening a gap in the Union center.

It was serendipitous that the desperate Confederates made their move just then.

Chapter 41

"Get in line." The First Sergeant were shoutin', pushing and shoving on the boys around me. We was sheltered from the Yankee fire by a low hill. Still hear the cannon. Pop of muskets was quieter, except on our left.

I was glad to be up and movin', I was so damn cold. But I was a bit uneasy, never havin' been in a real battle before. There was a lot of sortin' out, men milling here an' there and I was looking for Walter. Officers trying to get the men in order.

Young Wilbur Smith was laughin' like he was goin' to the dance, all eager. Slapping people on the back. Another fool.

I found Walter. He was right quiet now. His eyes looked scared. I thought that was about right, but I tol' him we was going to get us some Yankees. It sounded good. Wanted him to be confident. To be honest, I didn't feel it. Always thought I was as brave as the next fellow. Now I was wondering.

Just then we heard a lot of yellin' on our left. Couldn't tell whether it was us or them doing the yellin', but our officers seemed uneasy, so it weren't too good.

Colonel Green, he rode right up to speak to us. We got to hear him 'cause we was close. He held us in them weird eyes of his. Almost like we could see his soul.

Sayin' how we was gonna make a big push at the center of the Yankee line. It was real important 'cause there was more of them than us and we needed to do it now. "Boys, I want those Yankee cannons!" That Green, he's a right stirrin' man to listen on. Brave too.

Pyron comes over to us after Green rides away. I like Major Pyron. Won't have us do nothin' he wouldn't do hisself.

"Men, listen close," he says. "There's artillery in front of us. We have

500 yards to cross. I want you to spread out at arm's length in line as we move forward." He spreads his arms out. "They'll be firing round shot at us first. Then canister as we get closer. Maybe 200 yards."

Can't say that sounded too good.

"When you see one of their guns flash," he says, "you fall to the ground damn fast. Then you got maybe a minute to get up. You can move quick. There's not too far to go. No sense firing those shotguns 'til you get within fifty yards or so, so don't you bother. Keep moving." Pyron's face was hard. Breeze snapping at his words. "I want you to take those guns away from them Yankees and turn 'em around on 'em. You hear?"

We was all a cheerin' then. Even got me stirred up.

"Now move out and form up in a line and let's get at 'em," he said.

We come out from behind the hill and I cain't see nothin'. All kinds of trees and brush in the way. We went maybe 100 yards before we mounted a hill and I seen the Union lines.

We was walking in line like Major Pyron said. About a yard apart. Close enough so I could see the sweat on Walter's face. Wasn't hot. Not outside. He was on my right, our Lieutenant, Wesley Jones, from next town over to ours, was in front of us. There were about 700 of us, I'd guess. Three groups, we being the first. I'd a just as soon been the second.

First Sergeant was walking along the end of our line making sure no one fell behind. Only a few musket shots from the Yankees so far.

It started to snow kinda light. A pretty day all in all. I was so thirsty, I stuck my tongue out and a wet flake landed on my tongue. I was lookin' up. Didn't see the carcass of the horse I stumbled on and fell flat on my face. A good thing too 'cause just then one of their cannon flashed and a ball whizzed over my head.

There was lots of our dead horses and mules about. I see a good deal of walking in my future unless we could steal some back.

I felt warm now. The sun had come out. We was about 200 yards from the Yankees when our men started to drop. I saw Pyron out front of us, turning back and waving his sword. He was talkin' but I wasn't hearin'.

Grass was about two feet high here. I was right glad it was too cold for snakes. I don't like snakes much.

It was hard, being all take for us and no give. We was still too far away to use our shotguns.

Wilbur Smith turned towards me as if to say a word. Then his knees buckled and he sank to the ground. I could see blood on his mouth. Made a gurgling sound. Who was gonna tell his mama? Who was gonna tell anyone's mama, a thousand miles from home? I wondered if Walter was as scared as I was. 'Spect he was. I mumbled a prayer or at least those words I could remember.

I looked around at Walter and he seemed to be okay, moving fast. Man to our left was shot through his thigh. Ball musta hit somethin' 'cause he started spurting blood. Fell down cryin'.

Couldn't stop. Not there. I was rubbin' my thumb back and forth on the stock of my shotgun. Clutchin' it across my chest. I think I mighta run away if Walter weren't there.

First Sergeant shouted at me. "Stay in line, Davis."

Every time the cannon flashed I hit the ground hard, usually on a rock. I had bruises all over. Then I got up and ran like hell. Funny thing. I could smell the gunpowder real clear.

Seen a cannon ball bounce between the legs of ol' Clay Butt. You should'a watched his face, jaw ahangin' open. That boy is a lucky one.

Sometimes there was a cottonwood to hide behind and if there was, I hid. I was still itchin' something fierce. Damn lice. You'd a thought they'd had the good sense to stay home. Here I was runnin', fallin', and scratchin'.

One of our cavalrymen lay moanin' on the ground. Eyes staring off. Callin' out for water. Dead horse by him with his leg clean torn off. Nothin' I could do for him. I got no water.

Our Lieutenant fell, screaming, blood all over his jacket. I seen everything clear. But I thought about Becky and how I ain't had a letter and what that meant. I didn't want to think about getting shot. I felt like I had been out there bein' shot at two, three hours already, but that didn't seem likely.

Walter fell over and I started towards him. He must'a slipped 'cause he got back up quick. I was shoutin' to him, "You watch out." But he was watching close, so I pretty well took care of myself.

That's when I felt this pluck at my shirt which was hangin' out of my pants from my throwing myself around. I looked down and there was a hole clear through it. It was the only shirt I got, and it made me real upset, havin' it tore like that. Then I thought some about it. Another little bit and I'da been tore. That didn't do much to make me feel better.

About 100 yards away we started crawlin'. That was good 'cause the grass hid us and the guns couldn't get to us no more. They was firing over us at the boys behind. I could smell the water from the river. I sure wanted to get me some. I was thirsty as hell.

We could see the Yankees now. One of 'em had a dirty face. Either that or he was a greaser. Our boys was firing and some of the Yankee gunners started falling. I waited to get closer. I crawled towards a little sand hill I could see.

The Yankees 'round the guns must'a got scared, I guess, 'cause they started running. A Yankee officer was waving his sword, tryin' to stop 'em. I propped my shotgun on top of that sand hill and shot him in the belly. Shotguns weren't good beyond fifty yards, but up close it did the job. Doubled him over. I could see his eyes go wide as he went down. Mouth was open but he weren't sayin' nothin'.

First man I ever killed close up. Strange thing. I don't hate Yankees. Supposed to, but I don't. I felt kinda bad. But you gotta do it in a fight.

I rolled over on my back and saw to my reloading. We were all firin' now, the Yankees runnin' like there was a fire on their tail.

Some of our boys stood up and got at their gun. They stepped over the fellow I killed. His eyes was still open. A few of the boys fell, but they got the gun turned around.

By that time, the Yankees were wading into the river and I got one with my shotgun. Hit him across his shoulders. Pretty much blew his back apart. He fell over with a grunt. There was streaks of red in the water. Them Yankees could run, I'll say that for 'em.

Walter and me, we jumped up and took off runnin' after 'em, down our side of the river. Yankees runnin' for the river all down the line now. Scared as hell. We was yellin' and screechin'.

We must'a gone a quarter mile chasin' them Yankees. Couldn't get at 'em across the river. That's when I seen this Yankee officer ride up on t'other side with a white flag. I should'a shot that Yankee, 'cause Colonel Green, he agreed to a truce to tend the wounded. Just when we had 'em running. Could'a chased them all the way back to Fort Craig.

We spent all night out on the field. Thank goodness I finally got me some water. Had time to cook some bread and pork too before me and Walter was ordered to go on out and find our wounded boys. It was a cloudy and cold night. Must'a been way below freezin'.

I was shivering in my thin shirt, even with my blanket wrapped around my shoulders. I let Twitchel come on out with us. He'd come back after all the shootin' stopped. Runnin' up and down. He'd come nosing around, waggin' his tail.

I heard men moanin'. Hard to find the wounded in the dark. No moon. So black couldn't see nothin'. Heard more than we saw.

"Water. Please, some water." Off to the left a yard or two.

I found a Yankee boy leaning with his back against a cottonwood. He must have been around twenty. A boy like us. He died as I tried to give him a drink. I called out for a Yankee so he could be buried. I took his coat first.

Yankees give us shovels to bury our dead. Shared their medical supplies too. We didn't have none, our wagons bein' off somewhere. Got to say this though. We tended theirs and they tended ours.

We knew we won. And we took their cannon. I felt mighty proud of my first fight. I leaned down and scratched Twitchel behind the ears. "Good boy," I says.

Chapter 42

Old Chas was sleek and well-groomed. He was Canby's favorite horse and Canby was riding him on the far side of the river, parallel to his line. Old Chas pulled left sharply against the bit in his mouth and Canby was struggling to curb him when he saw the Confederate charge.

He wheeled and galloped to the riverbank ordering men forward to reinforce the left flank of McRae's battery. He saw McRae fall in front of his cannon. The New Mexico Volunteers were the reserves on the left. He didn't trust them, but he had no choice. There wasn't much time.

Juan Gimarez was just nineteen years old. Tall and skinny, he had been a boy on a farm near Socorro when he had been forced into the army. He had never fired a gun at another man. His sergeant shoved him and he stumbled forward at the top of the riverbank.

Gimarez came face to face with a shouting horde of Texans, apparently oblivious to the shell and canister falling around them. They were so close. He could see rage on their stubbled faces. Their mouths were twisted into ugly shapes. And they came on.

The man next to him fell screaming. It was too much. He dropped his old musket and ran. His friend Ramon Sanchez saw him run. He ran too. Then more. The entire left side of the Union line collapsed.

Juan Gimarez reached the river running as fast as he could. The shouts behind him now were louder. He waded into the river. The water slowed him.

The shotgun blast that caught him hit him full across the back. It tore out his lungs. He was dead by the time he hit the water, his black hair swirling in the current. A streak of red briefly pointed to the spot, then drifted away.

Canby was horrified as the volunteers turned to flee. He urged his horse into the river and waded forward among the retreating men. "Turn around!" he shouted, waving his sword. He slapped at men with the flat of his sword. "We must protect the guns." All to no avail.

Captain Benjamin Wingate's troops came up quick time on the Confederate left and started to pour musket fire into the massed Rebels. A shell exploded near Wingate and he dropped, throwing his troops into confusion. They fell back as more Confederates arrived to reinforce the first wave.

The Second New Mexico Volunteers had escorted the Union wagon train. Almost 600 men held in reserve on the far side of the river. Roberto Homero was among them. He was a brave man. He had never been in battle but he was prepared to stand his ground.

The Second New Mexico heard the boom of the artillery and the snap of small arms fire. But they couldn't see because of the cottonwoods on both sides of the Rio Grande. So the first fleeing men took them by surprise. Men suddenly appeared running out of the smoke and dust. Loose horses, wild with fear, got in among them. Then more men appeared, looks of terror on their faces, incoherent and trembling. It was the face of hell. Roberto Homero was not aware when his horse bolted for the rear.

On the left, Raguet's battalion had been driven back again. There were just too many Yankees. He had fought his men well, yielding the ground cottonwood by cottonwood. But they had run out of time.

Now he desperately positioned his men in their final defensive position. It was hopeless. He had sent to Green for reinforcements again and again. No one had come. The next Yankee onslaught would push them out. Then the Yankee artillery would enfilade the Confederate lines and it would be a slaughter. Then, suddenly, the Yankees pulled back.

Canby tried to reposition his right flank to cover the retreat to Fort Craig. His courier found Kit Carson within a few moments. Carson was the hinge of the assault, pressing Raguet on the Confederate left, unaware of the disaster on his own flank. Hasty words were exchanged. Carson pounded his hat against his leg and shouted. But he was exposed.

His bugler sounded the retreat. Eight companies fell back and melted into the bosque at the lower ford of the river that had been so hotly contested that morning.

Raguet waited for the Yankees. They didn't come. The silence was eerie. He put out men to find out what was happening. The Yankees weren't there.

The horses strained against the leather harness to pull the heavy Confederate guns forward the 700 yards to the Rio Grande. The heavy caissons bounced and shivered over the rough ground.

"Get those guns unlimbered!" Captain Trevanion Teel shouted, his heels skidding as he dismounted even as his horse still surged forward. "Load shell not round shot." The words came out ragged. He was winded. "Hurry, damn it, hurry. They're getting away!" he shouted, his voice hoarse with frustration, adding his weight to push the mouth of a gun around towards the retreating backs of the Union soldiers.

Union soldiers managed to form a skirmish line on the other side of the river. They held back the tide. For just long enough. Daylight was fading.

Canby rode, his shoulders rounded from exhaustion. The road back towards Fort Craig was crowded with soldiers. Some moving at random. The regulars formed up when they could find their company.

Wounded were everywhere. Most of the Second New Mexico had simply disappeared.

Green and Scurry were conferring behind the Confederate lines. Scurry was jubilant, flushed with victory. "Let's get after them. If we push 'em, we can take the fort."

Green shook his head. "The men are exhausted. We worked 'em hard. I don't think they can do it. It's nearly dark. We got no horses and Raguet's a mess. Let 'em go."

The two men looked up at cheering on the right. Three Union officers bearing a white flag, escorted by a happy group of Confederate cavalry, dismounted in front of them.

"Colonel," a Union Captain said, saluting Green. "Colonel Canby sends his respect, sir, and requests a two-day truce to tend the wounded."

Green nodded his assent as Scurry frowned.

Canby had no idea of how many effectives he had left. It had been a disaster on the left. A day later and he still didn't know. Stragglers kept coming in. Fort Craig bustled, but the men spoke in murmurs. He had dismissed two companies of volunteers. Better they should be gone. Clearly, he couldn't attempt another attack. Even if he knew where the Rebels were.

A council of war sat around the table in his smoky room. Roberts, Carson, Duncan. A bottle of whiskey was half finished. Duncan put his glass back down on the table and looked deep into the brown liquid. He held his tongue for now. He knew some of the officers had been calling Canby incompetent. He didn't know what he thought. So, he didn't talk.

"With the battery of cannon they took from us, Sibley could attack the fort," Roberts said. "That's what I'd do." He hit the table with his fist. "Otherwise, we'll be across his supply lines and at his back. He can't risk that."

"I think Sibley will make for Albuquerque or Santa Fe. Seventy-five miles. He can be there in a week, maybe less if he divides his forces." It was Carson. He took another swallow of his whiskey. "He'll need supplies. He lost half his wagons." Carson looked around him, disgusted. "This place sure stinks." All of the families along with the farm animals and the beef herd had been crowded into the fort.

Canby wasn't listening. This had been going on for the last hour. He was staring at the flickering lantern.

Damn it, could I have done anything different, he thought. If only. . . If only. It was such an important part of war.

Now he wasn't sure what to do. Was he losing his confidence? He ran his hand through his thick hair and his teeth ground the unlit cigar in his jaw. Best to take the middle ground. He removed the cigar and spat on the dirt floor before he spoke.

"Send a rider to Albuquerque. Warn them to send out pickets. If the Confederates come that way, I want all the supplies burned." His voice was stronger than he felt. "I want another rider to go to Fort Union and advise them of our circumstances. Tell them we'll be available to reinforce them if they're attacked but for now we're staying here." He was thoughtful.

The next sentence was almost a reflection. "We can't protect Santa Fe, but we need be prepared to defend Fort Union. We can't let it fall into Sibley's hands." He felt like he needed to do something positive. "And send Lord's cavalry to see if he can reestablish contact with the Rebels. I need to know what they're up to."

It was a dark night. Canby felt very much alone.

Chapter 43

I got me some shoes. Took 'em off a dead Yankee. Asked him nice. Fellow didn't seem to have a lot to say. I was pleased 'cause a lot of us is barefoot, Walter is. And we was asked to give up our horses. Maybe *asked* ain't the right term.

Boys found some Yankee rucksacks full of food near the river where we been fightin'. Dropped in a hurry by some Yankee boys, I figure. We ate good for once, bread, good pork, and some beans, which was all as well 'cause word was we didn't have hardly no rations left. And it were winter here where there weren't hardly much even in summer.

After bein' out all night, Walter and me, we were hunkered down by the fire. We was bone-tired. I had picked up a Yankee rifle and I was sittin' oiling it. I turned towards Nat Chessy, one of our boys from a farm near to ours.

"Nat," I says. "You find any miniballs that'll fit this here gun? You have any, I'll maybe trade you my shotgun." I already got me gunpowder and percussion caps. But them miniballs ain't balls of lead like ours. They's hollow, pointed pieces of lead made specially for their rifles, I suppose. Hear they're a heck of a lot more accurate than any muskets we got.

But Nat, he's kinda slow in the head. He looked at me like he didn't know what I was saying.

"I'd like your shotgun," he says. Shook his head kinda with his mouth ahangin' open.

"Don't make no difference whether you'd like it or not, Nat, less you found some lead'd fit this rifle."

Nat shook his head, says slow-like, "Nope, ain't found none of that, but I'd sure like your shotgun."

Good thing Sam Belcomb come skitterin' up. I didn't know what else to say to Nat.

"You got some water?" Belcomb says.

"No," I says back. "You go down to the river and get some yerself." We got water but Belcomb ain't no friend of ours. "Belcomb, you got any miniballs?" He shakes his head as he turns and starts towards the river, maybe half mile away, dragging his feet. Walter, he coughs.

"You okay?"

"Yeah. Just a might cold," he says. Even though we got a big fire burning. Light on his face made his eyes bright.

"I got this here coat off a Yankee." I took it off and passed it to him. "You take it. I'll find me another one." I didn't think I would, what with the boys out picking clean the battlefield all morning, but Walter looked peaked.

The fire was flickering off the five boys in our mess. Used to be six yestiday. We'd sung up "Dixie" and every other song we know'd. Now we was just quiet. Even boys who knew how to read couldn't. Fires too big to get close to. It were a real cold night, down near freezin', if not below. At least the cold held down the stink of the latrines we'd dug a few yards away. Good for somethin'.

The regiment were spread out over a mile or two. Couldn't see a lot of fires 'cause of the trees and hills, but we got these strange reflections about.

Any case, I'm sittin' by the fire, roasting one side and freezin' t'other, mending my shirt where the bullet put a hole in it. When I find myself thinkin' about my dad. Actually, Walter's and my dad. We used to sit by the fire way out in the scrub in Texas when he took us huntin'.

He used to talk to us real quiet. I don't remember much of what he said, but I remember drifting off to sleep with him atalkin'. Dad, he weren't an easy man. Could be right mean when he was drinkin'. It's been tough for Ma raisin' all us kids. Pa was sure no help. Maybe that's why she was so ornery.

Twitchel put his nose in my lap. I absently scratched him behind the ears as I was thinkin' back. Pa was cheap. Wouldn't spend a nickel. Had to give him all the money we done earned. I thought to heck with that. I'm gonna keep what I make, or at least part of it.

Pa, he found out and tried to wup me, but I was a big fella. I knocked him down. He din't try to wup me after that.

Twitchel, he raised his head quick and stared off to the side of the fire. Give a bark and darted off into the grove of cottonwoods near us. I heard him crashing around in the underbrush for a while. Then it got quiet. Must'a caught hisself a rabbit. Think he'd share.

It was getting late, but we was only a couple of hundred yards from Colonel Green's tent. Officers gathered around there, talking loud, someone playing on a harmonica. I thought I recognized the song but couldn't quite say. I think they was drinkin' whiskey. I mean real whiskey, not like what we got when we could get it.

Wouldn't want to be an officer though. Don't have the learnin'. 'Sides, too many of 'em get theirselves killed. Yankees aim at them, just like we do. Anyhow, they was makin' a lot of noise. Happy we'da won, I 'spect.

General Sibley, he ain't nowhere to be seen. That's worrisome. Boys don't like it. We expect to see the General. See him up front. Maybe Sibley's a coward. Don't know.

Seen Green appear at the front of his tent, holdin' back the flap. He's a big man. Says somethin' I couldn't hear. He looked tense, even from here. Harmonica stops. The officers start to wander off.

I see our Lieutenant come back to his tent. Bob, his slave, opens the flap. That Bob's a funny one. Today, during the battle, he don't go and hide like the other slaves. He found hisself a spot near where we was, where he could watch the fightin'.

I seen the look on his face. Maybe more hate there for the Yankees than I have. Don't rightly know why, since them Yankees is supposed to be fightin' fer him. Can have him, far as I'm concerned. Can have all of them for the good they are.

Word is tomorrow we're headed up North t'wards Albuquerque. That'd be okay. I'm pretty tired of being out here. It'll be good to be in a town fer a while. Hope the talk is right.

Twitchel, he crept back up to me and put his head in my lap again. Blood on his muzzle.

"You have a good dinner, boy?" I says, scratchin' him. I felt the silence come over the camp more than I heard it. Twitchel don't say back, so I got my blanket spread out and figured on getting a bit of sleep. Yawned and stretched a bit. Thought maybe I should write a letter to Becky soon. Don't mean write. Ask Willy Leeds to write it for me's more like it. Don't figure it matters much. Don't even know if the letters get sent. We don't get any. We're out here lonesome.

I scratched at me some. Maybe we'll be on the move tomorrow, I thought, rolling myself up in my blanket. Then I remember I gotta walk. It weren't sweet dreams.

Chapter 44

Report to President Jefferson Davis
(written from the field near Valverde)
February 22, 1862

Sir,

It gives me pleasure to report to you of our great victory at Valverde. I originally hoped to invest Fort Craig, but I perceived that the
fort was well defended and while we, in my estimation, would have
succeeded, it would have unnecessarily depleted our limited resources.

Consequently, I chose to bypass the fort and seek a position that
would cause the Union forces to fight in the open field, depriving
them of advantage. Our Army executed this flanking movement, under the very eyes of the enemy, in good order. Our victory proves the
soundness of these tactics.

This victory opens the way to Santa Fe, and thence Fort Union.
Fort Union represents, I believe, a major obstacle to the success of our
endeavors. Its investment will provide the supplies this Army needs
to extend its campaign. I anticipate that our victory there will inspire
those who believe in our cause to rise and strengthen us further with
both supplies and men. I will then be in a position to pursue the strategic goal of conquering Colorado with all its attendant benefits to
our Confederacy.

Respectfully,
Brigadier General Henry Hopkins Silbey

The victory of the Confederate troops at Valverde was a godsend to

Jefferson Davis. Nashville had fallen, the capital of Tennessee, the first Confederate capitol to fall. And two large Union armies were marching on Shiloh Church, near the major rail center supporting the western Confederacy.

The pressure was almost unbearable. The costs were staggering and his resources were sparse and dwindling.

The news of Valverde was heartening. Davis finally felt he may have been right to authorize the campaign in New Mexico. He slept well that night for the first time in two weeks and dreamed of the gold of California.

Chapter 45

February 21, 1862
(Fort Craig, New Mexico)
The Military Journal of Colonel Edward Canby

I have ordered the retreat to Fort Craig following the action at Valverde. The native New Mexicans, while numerous, can no longer be looked upon as an effective fighting force. Their performance in the recent battle was totally unacceptable and led to the consequent reverse. I simply do not have enough regular troops. Volunteers from outside the territory are not forthcoming, although I have a report that a regiment will start shortly from Colorado, but whether they will arrive in time to be of assistance is doubtful, given the weather conditions in the mountains.

I have sent a letter to General H. W. Halleck which I have copied here:

> Sir,
>
> You will probably learn that we have had a most desperate and bloody struggle with the Texans and have retreated to Fort Craig. It is needless to say this country is in a critical condition. The militia has all run away and the New Mexican volunteers are deserting in large numbers.
>
> The conquest of New Mexico is a great political feature of the rebellion. It will gain the rebels a name and prestige over Europe and operate against the Union cause.
>
> If they succeed, these Texans will have large additions of volunteers to their command, allowing them

to seek to extend their conquest toward old Mexico and in the direction of Southern California. We are fighting two-to-one and laying down valuable lives upon this issue. I request that you send at once—lose not a day— at least two regiments of infantry and a battery of rifled cannon to Fort Union. These troops cannot serve the Government better than saving this Territory.

Respectfully,
Edward R.S. Canby, Colonel, RA

I fear that the Government does not take our cause seriously enough and will not provide what is needed to defend ourselves or will not do so on a timely basis.

Chapter 46

February 23, 1862
(Henry Sibley to his wife from the field near Valverde)

Dear Charlotte,

Command is lonely. I cannot adequately describe to you the pressure I feel in leading this Army. The responsibility rests heavily upon me. There is no one in whom I can confide. Few understand.

Even Tom Green now shuns me since I was unable, due to my illness, to participate in the fighting at the Valverde ford. I would have given all to be there, among my men. But delegation is the art of command. Good men led by good men.

I have explained my goals. It was I who conceived this strategically important campaign. It was I who persuaded a reluctant government to undertake it. My strength has always been that of imagination beyond the ordinary. Unfortunately, I could not get the supplies and equipment for which I asked. It has imposed a crushing burden on me.

There is so much to do to lead an Army. So many decisions that others should make, but do not. I believe there is jealousy felt by some of my officers. I fear that a few may be writing to our superiors behind my back, damaging my reputation and seeking to undermine me. It is discouraging and has taken a further toll on my health.

I admit it is difficult not to indulge in an occasional drink. It is the only relief I have from the physical and mental pains that plague me. But I am careful not to let it get out of hand.

You are always in my thoughts. I hope you are in good health and the children are well. I know you will be best settled with your sister for the duration of my campaign. We are moving constantly and the country is desolate. I enclose here $10 for something you desire. Please write to me soon. I remain,

Your faithful husband,
Henry

Chapter 47

March 9, 1862
The Personal Journal of Louisa Canby
(Santa Fe, New Mexico)

There is so much upset here. We are to be left behind. Edward has ordered the Army to fall back to Fort Union and abandon Santa Fe. He feels that after the defeat at Valverde the men cannot be counted upon to defend this city. Apparently, Santa Fe is difficult to defend because of its position and lack of fortification. He also hopes it will allow him time to secure reinforcements. I do not understand these things so I must accept them.

It is so very cold. The men are wrapped in all manner of coverings, part uniform and part anything else that comes to hand. Officers are struggling to retain men at their work, but I have overheard grumbling. The Confederates are said to be only a day or two away.

Edward believes that Fort Union is strong and well supplied. He says it can be defended. There are few roads through the mountains to the fort and he says that is important. I know he must be correct. I can see how it would make it difficult for the Confederates to get in. I am uncertain how our troops can get out. I do pray for Edward's safety. And pray God we will not be separated for too long. He is all I have.

While the officers' wives and children are left here, Edward assures me we will be treated with respect by the Confederates. I believe him, but in honesty, I cannot say I am not nervous. Particularly since Edward has ordered all excess supplies, weapons and ammunition to be hidden or burned. They must be denied to the enemy. I saw men digging deep ditches and unloading wagons. They are clever at concealing their work. But I fear it will anger our occupiers.

I hope that General Sibley is among the first to arrive. I remember the wonderful Christmas we had at Charlotte and Henry's home. He is such a gracious man. I know he will see to us. How curious that a friend can become an enemy so easily and then become something else again. I am angered by this foolish war and the pain it has caused.

I am responsible for all the officers' wives, of course. I will do what I can to ensure that we have adequate food and shelter. The children are our particular concern. They seem so bewildered. We will render what service that we can to the wounded boys, whether they be theirs or ours.

My, oh my, I do not know what the next days will bring. But I do have faith in God to protect us.

March 11, 1862
(Fort Craig, New Mexico)
The Military Journal of Colonel Edward Canby

The enemy will certainly attempt to capture Fort Union with its supplies and ammunition. General Sibley is seeking to live off the land. He now has extended supply lines and, it appears, limited stores from which to draw. He cannot pursue his campaign without renewed supplies and ammunition. He previously commanded Fort Union and he is well aware of its stores. It is strategically critical that he be denied them.

The Confederate forces now occupy Santa Fe. The city was indefensible and we abandoned it. I have left the officers' wives and children there. They will be safe and treated with respect.

I must make a judgment as to when General Sibley will most likely strike at Fort Union and his routes of advance from Santa Fe. The concentration of our forces will be important, since by all reports, we can field fewer men, at present, then the Confederates have to oppose us.

Of the three mountain passes through the Sange de Cristo range from Santa Fe, the southernmost, through Glorieta Pass, presents the least difficulty, and I judge it to be the most likely to be used by General Sibley to move a large body of men and equipment together with his supporting baggage train.

Consequently, I will establish a primary unit of 100 troops in the southern pass to delay any enemy force attempting to attack Fort Union and to alert the main body of my forces. I will establish a smaller unit in each of the other passes.

I have ordered that the remainder of the force and all of the artillery remain at Fort Union within a day's forced march of any of the passes. In this manner, I can assure our defense of Fort Union, even if somehow the Confederates slip past my outlying troops.

I anticipate being soon reinforced by additional volunteer units from Colorado and New Mexico. I have received word that these units have been raised and are on the march. Their arrival and disposition may be critical to my defense of Fort Union, although the quality of these volunteer troops has proved uneven.

I intend to remain in Fort Craig in order to interdict the Confederate supply lines and deny any attempt to resupply General Sibley. When General Sibley has committed his troops, I will march and attempt to attack his forces from the rear.

Chapter 48

A cold gust of wind blew snow into his face. Theodore Kincaid shivered inside his heavy campaign cape as he knocked on the door, trying to stamp the slush off his boots. It was the dead of winter, February 10, 1862

"Come."

"Sir," said Kincaid, coming to attention and saluting, "we have received orders to march to the support of Colonel Canby."

John Slough looked up from the papers he was reading in the flickering light. He took off his spectacles and put his thumb and forefinger to the bridge of his nose, leaning back. "Finally," he muttered.

Slough was a thick man in his early forties. His long face was bearded. The beard was peculiar. It was divided into two parts. Above an aquiline nose, he had intense green eyes that reflected his aggressive nature. Slough was a lawyer by training, not a soldier. He had given up his law practice to serve his country. He was used to having his own way and he wasn't one to shun confrontation.

In May, 1861, the Colorado territory had a population of less than 26,000, mostly men. They were concentrated around Denver or in the mining camps scattered through the mountains to the West.

William Gilpin had been appointed governor one month after the surrender of Fort Sumter, in South Carolina. He had found an active secessionist element and he immediately set about raising troops to save Colorado for the Union. John Slough was his first appointment as Colonel of the regiment he intended to raise.

By early autumn, 1861, 800 miners and dry scrabble farmers had volunteered. These were hard men who had lived a mean existence.

Gilpin ordered them to Camp Weld, two miles up the Platte from Denver. And there they sat. They were drilled and trained. But they sat.

Finally, hearing of Sibley's surge into New Mexico, Gilpin, overwhelmed with frustration, felt compelled to act. He wrote seeking permission to send his regiment in support of Colonel Canby. Then, he too waited.

Slough leaned forward in his chair and placed his hands face down on his desk. "Well, they finally paid some attention to us, Kincaid. It is about time."

He raised a fist to his mouth and coughed. He cleared his throat before continuing, a guttural, rasping sound. "Give my respect to Major Chivington," he finally said. "Tell him we want to march as soon as possible. All speed. The weather isn't going to get any better." It had been snowing for four days.

As Kincaid retired, Slough's eyes turned thoughtful. Lord, 400 miles through the Rockies with a wagon train and 800 men, in the dead of winter. He shook his head.

It was February 22nd. In intense cold, with the snow crunching under their boots, the companies of the Colorado Volunteers were finally on the march. Nothing had gone well. Wagons had broken down. Men had gotten into scuffles. Supplies were slow to arrive.

Now they were finally on the trail. But for Slough, the Rockies still cast a dark shadow.

The Denver Times
March 14, 1862

Our prominent citizen, Colonel John P. Slough, with his First Colorado Volunteers, having hastily departed Camp Weld, had been moving steadily South since February 22. He was joined at the Purgatorie River by the balance of his regiment, under Lt. Colonel Samuel Tappan, his second in command, from Fort Wise. We are told that news of the Battle of Valverde reached Fort Wise on March 1, but those troops had gone no further than Bent's Old Fort when Captain Garrison from Fort Union rode into their camp and urged upon them a most speedy advance.

Tappan's men were said to have left behind all but bare essentials and, traveling with utmost haste, pressed forward. On the day they joined Slough on the Purgatorie, they had marched 40 miles. Men collapsed to the ground and fell asleep as they lay.

North of the Red River, it is reported that the whole force was met by an ambulance bearing news that Fort Union was being threatened by the Texans. Col. Slough, a decisive commander, ordered that everything be left at the river save arms and ammunition and a pair of blankets per man.

Sergeant Joshua Egan, a tall, shambling man, was having trouble with the cow. The cow didn't seem to want to go out through the fence to the road, even though he was urging it to do so with all his might. Maybe it was the farmer's wife shouting at him from six feet away. A stocky woman with a few teeth missing. Strong arms though. Waving a broom.

He didn't like foraging. You made people mad and he was scared some farmer was going to shoot him. Jim Brewer of Company B had gotten a back end full of buckshot just yesterday. Couldn't sit his horse. To listen to him you'd think he was mortal injured. Egan pulled his coat tighter around him.

"You jackdaw, taking all we have. We're just poor farmers. Where are my children going to get milk?" the woman shouted.

He didn't know what a jackdaw was. He didn't think he wanted to inquire. He was a sensitive man. "You got another cow," he said. She snorted and tried to poke him with her broom. "I already give you a voucher so the Army'll pay you for your cow," Egan said. It didn't seem to make any difference to her.

He'd already explained it. He had his orders. Straight from Lt. Colonel Tappen. The First Regiment of Colorado Volunteers was making a forced march to save Fort Union from the Rebels. It was a vital post. The main Union supply depot in the New Mexico territory.

"We had to leave our wagons and supplies behind. There's almost 800 men, ma'am. They gotta eat." The wind blew away his words. Worst wind he had ever seen. Like a tornado. And cold as ice water. His ears were freezing.

She just didn't want to hear any of it. She'd beat him with her broom. He hadn't realized a broom could hurt that much.

It was March 10. They had been halfway to Fort Union from Denver City when they had heard about the great defeat at Valverde. The Confederates were moving on Santa Fe. Fort Union was under attack. The Regiment had voted to make a forced march.

"For the honor and prosperity of the Republic," Colonel Slough had said. Slough commanded the regiment. Slick enough. Didn't know if he was a fighter. But he sure wasn't popular with the men, being stuck up and loud.

"I'm really sorry, ma'am," Egan said again, while trying to shoo the cow along. He gave her a sad look. She sounded like his ma.

They marched hard. Eighteen miles a day. Their feet hurt. Their shoulders ached. Egan felt about ready to fall over. But they got to Fort Union. It was the eighteenth of March.

The men at Fort Union shouted and whooped as The First Colorado came over the hill. A half-mile line of men in all manner of shabby dress. Could have easily been Confederates, except they'd been told it was volunteers from Colorado. "Pike's Peakers" they were called. Hard men, used to hard conditions. Frontier folk.

Egan was toward the front as they marched up. It was cold. It was always cold. Clear, now that the retched wind had subsided. His feet hurt like blazes.

They were exhausted, but they were ready to fight. He surveyed the broad stretch of open ground surrounding the star-shaped fort with strong earthen walls. Where were the Rebels?

Colonel John Potts Slough rode tall and proud at the head of his regiment through the gates of Fort Union. He sported dark curly hair. His peculiar, divided beard that made him look like a Russian czar, a description that would have pleased his men if they had ever heard of a czar, or Russia for that matter.

He took the cheers of the Union soldiers as his due and dismounted in front of Colonel Gabriel Paul, the commander of Fort Union. He saluted and Paul returned the salute. Almost fifty, Paul had gotten a little pudgy and didn't cut a military figure, but he was a battle-hardened veteran of the Mexican war and a respected leader. His gray beard covered a soft mouth.

"Welcome, Colonel Slough. Your men are a blessed sight. I'm Colonel Gabriel Paul in command of Fort Union. There are reports that the Confederates have taken Santa Fe. We're expecting an attack any day."

Slough frowned. "We were told you were under attack already. My men and I have made a forced march for the last twelve days to relieve you."

"I'm sorry for that. Let me order that your men be taken care of immediately." Paul turned to the captain by his side but Slough interrupted him.

"My men are all mountaineers. They are accustomed to the most severe hardships. They don't need tents or supper. That will be entirely unnecessary. This march to them is no more than a ten-mile march to your troops."

"Damn the man," Joshua Egan said under his breath to the soldier next to him. He pulled at his pants where they were chaffing him. "We're worn to the bone and haven't had a decent meal in eight days. And he's bragging on us at our expense."

The wind had kicked up again. The walls of the fort deflected it a little, but it still cut through Egan and made him shiver. "I'll bet *he* gets a warm bed tonight and a hot supper." Egan spat on the ground. "While we're going to lie out all night without a mouthful to eat. Damn him to hell."

But Slough's next statement made Egan smile. He said to Paul, "I would appreciate your distributing three gallons of whiskey to every company if you can spare it. The men would like a drink."

Paul turned to the captain again. "Please see to it promptly, Captain." The captain saluted and turned away, motioning to the man beside him, ducking his head and giving orders in a low voice.

"Would you care for a drink in my quarters, Colonel Slough?" Paul said. "I can advise you of the tactical situation and perhaps get your advice."

"That raises a subject we need to discuss, Colonel," said Slough. "I've reviewed the records and my appointment to rank precedes yours. I think you'll find as the senior officer present, I'm in command."

A look of dismay escaped Paul's military demeanor. "I can't believe that is possible, Colonel Slough."

"It is a fact. And I hereby assume command."

"I must protest. I am regular Army. I have far more military experience."

"And I'm sure I'll find that very valuable in making my plans. Now, I would very much like that drink you mentioned. Shall we go?"

"I will write to Washington, Colonel Slough. This is completely inappropriate. And I must ask to see your commission."

"If you must," said Slough, taking Paul by the elbow and making a sweeping open-handed gesture. "Shall we?"

Chapter 49

"Damn it, man, you are disobeying a direct order. Colonel Canby specifically ordered me not to move from here until he advised me of his route and point of junction." Colonel Gabriel Paul was furious. He could not keep his hands still.

They were sitting across the table in Paul's spartan office. It was already dark. It got dark early in the winter. Paul hit the table with his fist causing the kerosene lamp to totter dangerously.

John Slough reached up to steady the lamp. "Please don't shout." His voice was calm. He actually gave a thin little smile. He found this funny. Slough was at ease now that he felt in control.

Paul was not. His lips were drawn up into a thin line. Blood suffused his face, giving it a red sheen. "I will not permit it. You cannot put this fort at risk."

Slough was amused. This simpleton was challenging him on a matter of interpreting a document. He stared at Paul with his dark, piercing eyes. "Those orders also require *me*..." he paused a moment to let the point sink in, "to harass the enemy by way of partisan operations while awaiting reinforcements. That is what I intend to do."

Slough also thought those orders were out-of-date, since they included the phrase, "while waiting for reinforcements." He had brought the reinforcements himself. Besides, the orders were addressed to Paul.

"You're taking all my men." Paul was having difficulty maintaining his composure. His statement was something of an an exaggeration, but, in fact, Slough proposed to take more than 1,500 men and most of the artillery, leaving the fort dangerously exposed, in Paul's judgment.

"Colonel Paul, I propose advancing to Bernal Springs," he said, pointing to a map spread on the table between them, just forty-six miles. "As you can see, I will be interposed along the Santa Fe Trail between Fort Union and Santa Fe. Any Confederate advance must go through Bernal Springs. And in any event I will be in a position to support you if required."

Which was true, more or less. Paul thought that even forty-six miles was beyond the distance of effective immediate support, but he didn't think Slough would stop at Bernal Springs since he intended to "harass the enemy." He was dealing with an amateur. And he suspected a man whose ego far exceeded his ability. It could be a disaster. He had a sinking feeling that it would indeed and that he would somehow be held to blame. It would end any hopes of advancement.

"I've made up my mind," finished Slough. "I believe that this is the most effective strategy." He folded the map and rose.

Paul concluded that it was hopeless to try to change Slough's mind. He clinched his fist. The man was arrogant beyond words. He wouldn't listen to advice. But, damn it, he was the senior officer. Paul had confirmed that. Slough's commission was dated a matter of days before his own promotion. He had already complained to Washington, but an exchange of letters would take months.

"At least leave me Captain Lewis's command and two sections of artillery to protect the fort."

"I'm sorry. I believe it would be safer not to split my forces in so inappropriate a manner."

My God, he thought, the man talks as if he knew what he was saying. "This disaster will be on your shoulders," Paul said. "I shall write Washington." Paul did not bother to mention that he had already written once.

"If the Confederates are no stronger than reported by our scouts, the troops under my command will be sufficient to control their action and to defeat them in case of attack," Slough replied calmly.

Scouts had reported two days ago on a reconnaissance of some Confederate forces in the area. It was uncertain as to the Confederates size or intent.

But it didn't matter. Two days was forever, Paul thought. Besides, in his experience, intelligence wasn't trustworthy. Certainly not to be relied upon. Useful only to help a commander make a decision based on his understanding and feel for the strategic situation. What understanding did this man have?

"I don't want to discuss this further. We are going to march tomorrow at noon." Slough executed a military like turn on his heel and walked out, leaving Paul in a state of suppressed fury. Feeling helpless always did that to him.

Paul went to the door. "Captain," he shouted gruffly. The captain rushed to the door. "Send a rider to Colonel Canby. Tell him that John Slough of the Colorado Volunteers has asserted his seniority and assumed command." Weir scribbled on his pad. He licked the pencil point as Paul continued, "In defiance of your orders, he intends to set out to meet the Confederates between here and Santa Fe, leaving Fort Union dangerously undefended. He has taken our artillery." The captain looked up to see if there was more. "That's all. Hurry, damn it." It would take four days to even hope for a response. Far too long. Well, he had done what he could.

March 21 was going to be a big day for Colonel Slough. He was finally in command of an army about to face the enemy. And he was going to prove himself in battle. He knew how it would burnish his name. He might even run for governor.

Sergeant Joshua Egan of the Colorado Volunteers had had a restless night. Twelve miles wasn't that long a march, but they had settled into camp at the village of Loma and most of the men had been hallowing with the women and fighting with the greaser men all night. The soldiers had been told to stay out of the village, but no officer was going to keep them away from liquor and women. It had kept him up. Egan was cranky.

He turned towards Jeff Muffit who was trudging alongside him. "You look like you been rode hard and put down wet. You get in a fight with a bobcat or somethin' last night?" There were scratches on Muffit's face and a small cut above his eye crusted with dried blood.

"I don't wanna to talk about it." Muffit wiped at his mouth with the back of his hand.

"Well, why not?" Joshua got some small satisfaction in pushing at Muffit, since Muffit had come back stumbling into camp in the middle of the night and awakened him.

"My head hurts." He squeezed his bloodshot eyes together. It didn't do any good.

"From the outside or the inside?"

"Both. Shut up."

"Why that's not right sociable of you, Jeffrey. You and me, we're friends, ain't we?"

"Joshua, I told you. Don't talk. It hurts my head. And I think I might a gotten something from one of those Mexican whores. I'm itching like hell." He reached down and scratched roughly at his crotch and sighed.

"How far you think we got to walk today? I got to get me some sleep," he said. "Maybe see the doctor."

"Don't know. All I know is what I was told. Same as you was told. We're going to Bernal Springs to see us about some Rebels." Joshua cocked his head. "You think they're near as fierce as they say?"

"Naw. That's talk." Muffit hoped. He'd never been in a battle. Never even killed a man.

They marched nineteen miles along the Santa Fe Trail the next day, much to Jeff Muffit's distress. And seventeen more the day after.

They bivouacked outside of Bernal Springs on the morning of the 24th of March. It was a flat plain covered with scrub. Good water. Joshua wasn't exactly exhausted. But he felt like he'd used his legs hard.

The men voted to name the bivouac Camp Paul, in honor of the red faced, irritated, once and present commander of Fort Union. A grand joke.

They liked John Slough pretty much now, except when he was still a pompous ass. At least they liked him more than they liked that regular army officer. One of their own. They chortled and punched at each other until it got dark. Cold and dark.

The Lieutenant came by. "Egan and Muffit. You got first picket duty. Stay sharp. We don't know where Johnny Reb is."

Well, damn. Just damn.

Everyone else in the Company pitched their tents. They lit their bonfires. And waited.

Chapter 50

I shor don't know how our dang officers find so many mountains fer us to climb when there's all that river valley out there. We was in the Sandia Mountains on our way towards Santa Fe when I, Ezra Davis, performed perhaps the bestest feat of the war.

Wore out a whole Yankee company of cavalry like they was about to die. It were a sight to behold. Can't understand how old Jeff Davis, no kin, didn't send me a commission. Must'a forgot.

Anyways, I'd been given a horse for the occasion. Actually t'was a mule. More actually, a mule I done stole one night from a Yankee camp. I crawled over on my belly past their campfire and got in among their horses. It was real dark and I was afraid of interruptin' their festivities, so I ended up with this here mule. Ornery fella.

Me and my detail of three boys was loyally doin' our duty of scouring the countryside for provisions. They was sparse that particular day.

Me and the boys clip clop up a wooded trail to the top of a hill to see what we was about. Pretty country if you're partial to mountains and trees. Me, bein' a Texas boy, I like to see what's out front a me.

What was out front a me on the next hill, 'bout two miles away, was a whole company of Yankee cavalry. They looked at us. And we looked at them, decidin' whether to fight.

Now some say you don't rightly ask how many, but only where your enemy be. I don't cotton to that theory myself. Me and my three boys didn't like the odds all that much, so when the Yanks came galloping down their hill, we done charged full speed down the backside of ours.

Now mules is hearty, but they ain't fast. And the other three boys, they had horses. Over the first mile or two the Yankees closed the ground between us pretty well. It was getting a bit hot.

144

I was a spurrin' my mule like all get out. I didn't think that damn mule wanted to be reclaimed by the Union. That mule didn't know he could run so fast. I'm leanin' forward and giving him the what fer. Bullet whizzed over my head.

People shooting at me gives me an incentive like. While I didn't think the Yankees could hit the side of my house from a galloping horse, I think too much of my hide to test the proposition too close.

Them a chargin' and us a chargin' too, only in the same direction, I could feel 'em breathin' on me. Rabbit skittered out onto the trail. I could see its pink eyes. It looked about like I felt. Turned and high-tailed it back into the brush.

Must'a made ten miles quick like that, when we come around a bend poundin' along straight into the arms of Company A of John Shropshire's Regiment on their way to meet up. Never been so glad to see such a mangy bunch in all my life.

I turned and waved my hat at the Yankees who had reined up some distance back. I'da turned and charged 'em, but I thought my mule might be tired. I'm an animal lover.

That night I slept pretty well, bein' back with my company. We'd fin'ly moved out from Albuquerque. Sweet stay. Almost two weeks. General Sibley took his time, but I guess he knows best. I actually got to sleep in a house. We all got a real belly full a whiskey.

Also, me and the boys liked being 'round women, even if they was Mexican women. Some of 'em was right accommodatin'. Particularly this dark haired, kinda plump one that took a likin' to me. But I don't talk about them things, nor about her husband chasin' me barefoot through the streets, wavin' a meat chopper until we run upon some other of our boys. Which reminds me, I got to have another letter writ to Becky.

We was to rondevu with Major Pyron near where the Santa Fe Trail enters the mountains. *Rondevu*, that's a military term like. Means meet up. I heard an officer say it.

Since I'm thinkin' of bein' a lawyer when this war is all over, I listen pretty close. Some lawyers among the officers. It shouldn't be too hard bein' a lawyer. They don't do nothing I can see.

Pyron, being the brave fighter he is, hears that the Yankees are goin' to attack Santa Fe, which we done taken when them yellow-bellies run. So, he ups and rides to meet them in the mountains. That's what I heard Lieutenant Willims say to another lieutenant I din't know. Green, he orders us to meet up with Pyron to even the odds a little. So, we lit out.

I'm back to walkin' again. Damn mule died. Yankee mules, they got no sense. After our little stroll in the mountains, I let him loose and he finds a spring and drinks 'til he keels over. Guess I'll have to steal another one, first chance I get.

It's snowin' and so cold my ears is trying to tuck themselves in. It bein' the twenty-fifth of March you'd think it'd get warmer soon. But it don't. I tell you, I wasn't cut out for this here life. I were born to be a man of leisure. Don't right know how this happened.

There was lots of buzzards circling in the air. Don't know why, maybe a dead deer. But it weren't a good omen.

We finally makes camp about fifteen miles below Santa Fe. Walter an' me and two others had a big campfire. Drew our rations and started to cook our bread. Takes about fifteen minutes to cook it right.

There's somethin' good 'bout being in the open country at night. It's quiet. I mean, not quiet. There's lots of small animals and Twitchel's always chasin' after them, making a racket. And there's owls at night. But the sounds kinda blend in.

I like to look up at the sky and see them stars. Someone once tol' me there's patterns up there. Pointed one out. Forget which. But I just like to look at 'em.

Our Cap'n, he tells us we was waiting for Major Pyron to see what the Yankees is up to. He says we goin' to continue along the Santa Fe Trail into the mountains.

We was to make sure none of them Yankees from Fort Craig hits us from behind. Makes sense. But I do hate the waitin'. I hate the fightin' to, but at least it ain't borin'.

Walter's still coughing a might. I don't like that. Been to the doctor. Said he can't do nothin' about it. We been losin' too many men. He gives him some syrup stuff. Tells him he's not sick enough be to sent back to Santa Fe.

I think I'm goin' to get me to bed early if my damn lice would stop eatin' at me. I got a feeling things is goin' a get a might hot when Pyron flushes out the Yankees. I guess we'll see.

Chapter 51

March 20, 1862
The Personal Journal of Louisa Canby
(Santa Fe, New Mexico)

How strange this is. We are here in Santa Fe among the enemy. The uniforms are different, but beyond that, it is like being in Monterey, but with a sense of underlying unease.

The officers are respectful. When I see one on the street, he doffs his hat and says, "Ma'am." The ordinary soldiers are rowdy and not as clean as Union boys, but they are volunteers, so what can be expected of them? We see them only on the street, and they are perfectly polite.

It is very cold. We have adequate wood and our houses are warm. We busy ourselves with sewing and talk. We also assist with the sick when we are needed. There is one man, an old Negro, that the Confederates refuse to treat. We have done our best for him, although several of the wives did object. They were afraid the Confederates might punish us. But we have no medicine. Fortunately, the Confederates tolerate us doing so, but barely. He seems to be getting worse.

During winter, there are not so many boys that fall ill. It seems as though the warm weather acts to spread disease, particularly among the ordinary men who live more closely together.

There was no fighting here. The mayor of the town was in the main square to surrender the City when the Confederates arrived. Some people were turned out of their homes in order to house the Texans, but it was done with great politeness, so long as there were no objections. The officers even ordered men to assist the families in moving. Of course, there was some disturbance when the soldiers collected all the available food and supplies from the people and the shops. But we were left well provided for and we are grateful.

The commander here is Colonel Scurry. He paid us a visit almost as soon as he rode in with his troops. Colonel Scurry assured us that we were welcome in his city. I asked him about General Sibley. He seemed rather curt. He said he did not know when, or even if, Henry would come to Santa Fe. It was a disappointment. I had hoped to see Henry.

But Colonel Scurry did invite all the wives of the senior officers to dinner at his headquarters. It was a fine meal with ham and beef. There was a quail soup, and many puddings and other desserts. He even had wine.

The entire dinner was served by Negros. Colonel Scurry treats them as we would our Mexicans, politely but firmly. They all seem content. It makes me wonder at this war.

There has been great activity these last days. Shouting and a great deal of noise. It seems as if the Confederates are preparing for an expedition. Wagon, upon wagon is being loaded with supplies and food. It is difficult for me to accept that they are setting out to harm Edward, but I know that must be the case.

We have no choice but to accept our situation and await word of the outcome of whatever battles will be fought. I wish these people no harm. They have been generous to us. Yet I know men will be killed and wounded, and I do hope for a Union victory. So, we float on a sea, with no land in sight, helpless to direct our ship. It is most unnerving.

Chapter 52

We hadda walk guard 'round the camp fer two hours at a time. Damn hard for some of the boys with bare feet on that frozen ground.

Thank goodness, I got me them shoes. Though, truth be told, the soles were fallin' off after marchin' with Pyron all the way to this place. Johnson's Ranch it's called. Act'ally, we was a few miles further on, Pryon wanting to get as fer as he could.

They say it's on the Santa Fe Trail. Don't know myself. But there's a trail up ahead through the mountains, so I guess they could be right.

Anyway, my feet was wet and cold in no time. Might as well have had no shoes at all.

I was right glad when the sun decided to bestir itself and it got a bit warmer. I rolled myself up into my blanket and went right to sleep, trustin' to our pickets.

Now our pickets at that time were Phillips' Company of Brigands, and a nastier bunch I ain't never seen. I think every cutthroat and thief in Mesilla must'a signed on. Can't say I liked them boys much. Me and Walter avoid sharin' their company as much as possible without givin' offense. I weren't sure in a pinch who they might shoot and I'd as soon be out of range.

So I'm sleepin' nice, when right sudden there's a lot of shootin' and people shoutin' that we're bein' attacked. Must'a been around noon, judging by the sun. I rolled out of my blanket and grabbed my shotgun. I still ain't got no miniballs for the rifle I found. Scared old Twitchell something fierce. Dog'd been sleepin' and I guess I rolled over on him. Gives out a yelp and scurries off into the woods.

Well, it looked to me like the whole Union cavalry was drawn up 'bout 400 yards away. We got ourselves into a ragged line using any handy tree or rock. Pyron and Shropshire went up and down our line, just as cool as you please, showin' us where they wanted us.

Walter, he was next to me, coughin' a lot.

"You don't look so good," I says. He just keeps staring straight ahead. "Why ain't you got on that Yankee coat I give you?" No reply. I reached over to give him a shake. Wouldn't you know, some Yankee shoots at me, and I feel this burn on the back of my right hand. Bullet ploughed a furrow in it. I felt damn lucky. I stuck my mouth around it and sucked on the blood. Felt okay. I wasn't goin' near any of them doctors.

I poked Walter again. He stirred. "Ezra, leave me alone," he says. "I'm so tired I just want to close my eyes. Up all night with this cough."

"You better watch out. You keeps coughin' like that and they knows just where to find you. Some Yankees liable to give you a good long sleep."

"Not so long as I stays behind this here tree," he says. "And that's just what I'm intendin' to do."

Right then there's this commotion on my left. Boys are shoutin' about the Yankees coming round us up the hill on our left. We gotta stop 'em or we'll be surrounded.

Walter stays put but I run that way, ducking behind trees and rocks as I go up the hill. The woods is full of blue-bellies and I let go with my shotgun but don't hit nothin' I can see. I shout for Jake Larkin to cover me so as I can reload, but old Jake was advancing to the rear in a mighty big hurry.

More and more Yankees is up there, coming around and I'm a squatting and pouring in powder and shot and rammin' it home. I get one barrel loaded when I see a whole mess of blue comin' my way.

Now, I'm as brave as any, but not foolhardy, and if it had only been six to one, no doubt I would have got out my Bowie knife and gone at 'em. But how's there eight or ten comin' down the hill, I'm lookin' for me a place to hide.

Well, there's this big rock about six feet away and I notice there's a deep hole to one side of it. I scurry that way, all crouched down, and throw myself under it, hoping there ain't no varmint sleepin' in there.

Anyway, I was okay. Smelled kind of like dead leaves. Nice and snug and out of sight. I just gettin' comfortable when, I'll be damned, someone else don't throw hisself in on top of me.

I says, "Hey, this here's my hidey hole. You go find your own. Ain't no room for two."

He says, "Scrunch down. Them Yankees is comin' down the hill and my legs is stickin' out."

Well, I scrunch and I scrunch and he wiggles in a bit. Then I hear a lot of shoutin' and commotion and this fellow flies back out from under the rock feet first, like he's carried on wings. But his wings is blue. I hear them sayin', "Lieutenant, come look see what we got here."

Meanwhile, I'm tucking in and balling up to be as small as I can be. My gun, damn it, scrapes the underside of the rock and an arm reaches down and grabs me by the collar.

This tall, thin Yankee, who don't look like two cents but is real strong, he drags me out and dumps me on the ground. Then he laughs and says to this other fellow, "Well, damn, maybe the whole yellow-bellied Reb army is hiding in there."

I don't appreciate that too much and I give him whatnot. But he pokes me with his sticker and I see the point of his argument.

I'm not lookin' forward to being a prisoner. No, sir. But I'm sure up against it, what with eight Yankees all around me looking fierce. And one having his bayonet pokin' my ribs.

A fellow comes over. I figure he must be the officer 'cause he's got on a coat with some gold things on the shoulders. He says official like, "Move aside men. Hand me his shotgun." I dropped it first thing out of the hole. Didn't want to give anybody the wrong idea. That's how I am. Good at communicatin'.

This officer, he takes my shotgun from the man who picked it up and looks it over. "Worthless," he says. He sounds disgusted.

Now I took that as an insult. My daddy used that gun. But I don't say nothin'. Then he done somethin' I don't hardly believe.

He grabs the barrel and hauls himself back, sayin', "Worthless," again, and swings it, stock first, against the rock.

Now my daddy weren't the smartest man I ever met, but he did teach me not to swing a loaded gun against a rock with the barrel pointed in your direction. Yes, sir. He did teach me that.

This gun goes off with a bang like to scare the bejesus out of everyone there. Blew a hole in that officer's belly and spattered me and everyone else with his blood. He lays on the ground holding his belly and crying. The Yankees were all a tryin' to help this fellow, callin' and runnin' this way and that.

In the meantime, no one's paying no attention to me and I'm a backing away, slow like, 'til I get behind a big tree. Then I lit out fast as I've ever run. I didn't look back. I crashed through a grove of cottonwood trees, running around this tree and that. I figured it would be harder to shoot at me in the woods. Wasn't necessary. Maybe they didn't think I was worth shootin'. I kept low through the brushy areas. But I kept goin'.

I stopped after maybe five minutes. I put my hands on my knees, breathin' real ragged. Felt like I tore some of my insides loose. I finally caught my breath. Looked around and I seen no one about. So I laid down on the ground and rested for a little.

It were quiet when I got up. So, I started walkin' in the direction from which I come, trying not to make no noise. Real nervous like. Going a couple of minutes, then stoppin' to listen.

Maybe it were an hour later, someone shouts at me. I can tell you I did give a jump. Thank the good Lord it was a Texas boy.

All in all, I didn't do too bad, even if it ain't been too good a day for us. Here I was back at the Johnson Ranch. I had some food in my belly. Walter were okay. Twitchel weren't nosing around. Where could that dog have got off to?

The back of my hand was hurting where I got shot. I hadn't given it a lick of thought all day. But now it stung me, so I chewed up some tobaccie and packed it into the wound. I heard that was the thing to do.

I could'a poured some of my whiskey on it. They'd given us all some. But I didn't wanta waste it.

I wrapped my hand up in a rag. It felt better. Now if the Yankees would have the common decency to let me get a night's rest.

Looks like I'll get to fight another day. Although I can't say I were lookin' forward to it none.

Chapter 53

Major John Chivington was smiling. His Colorado Volunteers had done well in their first fight. The Pike's Peakers had turned back the Confederates at Apache Canyon. Almost surrounded them. But he was puzzling at what to do now.

Chivington was a giant. Round faced and heavily bearded. An intense man. And he was immense. Over six feet four and closing in on 315 pounds. It made you sorry for his horse.

He was known as "The Fighting Parson." The minister of the Denver Methodist Church, he had been asked to become chaplain of the regiment. He held out for a line position. He wanted to fight, not preach.

He was pugnacious by nature. Why, in Platte Missouri, some folks didn't like his brand of religion and threatened to tar and feather him. Chivington ascended to his pulpit the next Sunday with two pearl-handled six shooters. Pearl-handled to do the Lord's work, he said.

He took out the pistols and laid one down on either side his bible and drew himself up. "Now, let's begin," he said. "Anyone out there who wants to take my place is welcome to try." No one did.

His men were scattered from the double enveloping maneuver he had executed so effectively. And he had a slew of Rebel prisoners he had to deal with. These arroyos in the canyon bottom and the wooded slopes he had used so effectively, now had become his problem. Ideal places to bushwhack a small Union force.

And he had his own dead to bury and his wounded to attend to. He took the truce the Rebels offered under the white flag borne by a young Rebel lieutenant.

He looked over to two of his aides and motioned them forward. This message was critical. "I want each of you to ride to Colonel

Slough. Advise him we need to be reinforced immediately. We are confronting a major Confederate force."

The two horses raised a dusting of snow as they galloped away. Chivington had no doubt messengers were heading the other way as well. It wouldn't be long now as the armies gathered. It only depended on who could move first.

The thought made him uncomfortable. He didn't have a good feeling about Slough. He wasn't a military man. Chivington didn't know if he was reliable. There was something that smacked of ambition about him.

"Lieutenant," he said, turning to another aide, "order the men to fall back to Pigeon's Ranch. We'll camp there tonight and wait for reinforcements."

It was four miles back to the ranch down the Santa Fe Trail. That much closer to Fort Union. Closer to reinforcements, he figured.

Pigeon's Ranch was located at one of the places on the Santa Fe Trail where the mountain canyon widens out into a narrow valley. It was a compound of low adobe houses and barns surrounded by adobe walls for protection. A good defensive position. It also had plentiful water.

Alexander Valle, the owner of Pigeon's Ranch, was a dedicated Union man. He'd do his best for Chivington. Chivington had heard he'd been nicknamed "The Pigeon" because of the manner in which he danced. The thought brought another smile to Chivington's rough features. He could see in his mind the skinny man dancing with his hands tucked up into his armpits.

The lieutenant had returned. He stopped and saluted. "I've given the orders to fall back, sir." Chivington grunted. It was starting to grow dark and the night was going to be cold. There was already snow on the trail. He hoped it didn't snow again and slow down the reinforcements.

His reinforcements had to come through the pass. The Rebels were on the plain past the mountains and would have an easier time of it. Another reason for withdrawing to Pigeon's. He looked around in the gathering shadows.

He turned to his lieutenant again. "I want a reinforced picket line set up, there and there and there." He pointed to his map. "I want to have plenty of notice if the Rebels come our way."

On the other end of the Santa Fe Trail, a plume of dust raised concerns among the 600 Confederate soldiers under Colonel William Scurry. They were encamped on the plain below the Sangre de Christos. One of the foraging parties had just brought in a little corn and a small herd of sheep and the men were roasting mutton over their open campfires. Food had been scarce and they were chattering and looking forward to their first full meal in several days.

"That ain't good," an old sergeant said, looking up. "Put the meat deeper in the fire. I got me a bad feeling about that," he said pointing at the approaching plume of dust. The men around the campfire muttered and cursed as they always did, but there was something keen about the way they spoke, as if it were a good thing.

The messenger reined in, saluted and handed Scurry the message. He unfolded it in his right hand and reached into his inside pocket for his glasses. He set the wire rim spectacles on his nose using both hands. The rough paper he was holding brushed against his face uncomfortably. He looked down at the message and turned it more towards the nearest campfire so he could make it out.

"The enemy has moved from Fort Union and is in full force in my front. I have a strong position. Will hold them at bay and await your arrival. Pryon."

Scurry scribbled a response and sent the saluting messenger galloping back. Then, hat in hand, he shouted down the line, "Pack up, boys, Major Pyron's been fighting a lot of Yankees and we must go to him."

There were two ways to go. The most direct way was north, straight to Johnson's ranch, maybe fifteen miles. Or he could head east along the Glorieta Mesa above the pass and come down on Pigeon's Ranch. Maybe catch the Yankees from the rear.

But the Yankees were probably in control of the canyon, he figured. So, he decided to go by the most direct route. It was a fateful decision, as it turned out.

The old sergeant, he was thirty-two, gingerly snatched a big piece of mutton from the fire and juggled it into a piece of pan bread. He rubbed another piece of bread over the greasy meat and stuck it in his mouth. Then he wrapped the mutton in a rag, picked up his pack and stuffed it in.

The old man picked his shotgun off the rock he had laid it against and joined the line of barefooted men going off down the snow-dusted trail into the mountains beyond, chewing on his piece of bread. A Rebel yell came from someone back in the line. The teamsters scurried behind them to break up the camp and pack the baggage train.

He licked his callused fingers one at a time. It was good to finally be on the move again. Tomorrow would likely see another fight.

Chapter 54

March 19, 1862
(Fort Craig, New Mexico)
The Military Journal of Colonel Edward Canby

I have just learned that, contrary to my orders, the Colorado Volunteers, together with many of our regular troops, under the orders of Colonel John P. Slough, have marched from Fort Union to meet the Confederates on the Santa Fe Trail in the Glorieta Pass.

Colonel Slough has taken all the artillery from Fort Union, leaving it virtually defenseless if the Confederate forces come through another pass in the Sangre de Cristo Mountains. I have ordered as many troops and guns as possible from Fort Craig to Fort Union but, at best, it will be ten days until they can reinforce the garrison there. I have assumed command of these troops and placed Captain Champlin in command of Fort Craig.

I intend to court-martial Colonel Slough as promptly as practicable. I pray he has not done irreparable harm to the Union.

Chapter 55

I was right bushed. What with fightin' all afternoon, then marchin' back to Johnson's Ranch. Even too tired to play poker, which is sayin' some. Didn't have no money anyways.

I was worried the damn Yankees might be settin' to attack us in the morning. There sure was a lot of 'em. The boys and me, we felt small here in our camp. Not like before. Pyron said he got us a truce 'til eight tomorrow morning, but them truces has been known to fall apart. I don't know that for a fact, but I guess it made me right skittery.

This war sure weren't much fun no more. Half rations can only take you so far, I says. We was always hungry. And truth be told, being shot at didn't do me much.

Pyron, he's a good man. Scurry and Green is first rate. Men you can count on. We wondered on General Sibley. Ain't seen hide nor hair of him for weeks. It ain't right. Some says he's alivin' it up back in Albuquerque, drinkin' and whoring. Don't know myself. Do know it's hard bein' out here alone. No news, no letters. I sure wonder 'bout Becky.

My hand's botherin' me where I got nicked. Like to throbbing. Chewed up some more tobaccie and packed it in, but it still hurt. Besides, Walter were coughin' with like a gurgle, and I couldn't sleep.

I poked him and he grunted and rolled over. Made him about as comfortable as I could. Give him my extra blanket and kept the raggedy one. Tucked it around him. Seemed like he had a fever. Not too bad, I thought. He kept movin'. All of us was sick, one way or t'other.

It was getting on towards midnight. Clear, but 'bout as cold as our ice house in the wintertime. I lay there listenin'. The camp was quiet, 'cept for a picket callin' out or someone cursin' when he tripped on a rock going to relieve hisself.

Lookin' up at a sky full of stars, cold nippin' at my ears while the fire glowed red to the coals. Reminded me of when I was a little boy and Pa took me huntin'. This were afore Walter were old enough.

Every once in a while, I'd see this streak of light. Asked Pa about that when I was knee high. Said it was God drawin' with his finger. Don't reckon I believe that.

The body lice seem to be getting worse. I was layin' there scratchin', thinkin' about why Twitchel hadn't come back when I heard a deep rumbling sound. Not so much heard it as felt it through my backside.

The sound of a lot of men movin'. I jumped outa my blanket like there were a snake in there with me. My foot got tangled up and I tripped. I never was too coordinated. Hit my elbow. It hurt like the dickens, but I muffled a curse.

I scrambled away from the fire, which was makin' a lot of noise, cracklin' and such, and brushed away some snow. Pressed my ear down on the ground. I could hear the tramp, tramp, tramp of feet. The clear ringing of some men with shoes on but also the soft sounds of bare feet. The Yankees all had boots.

I let me out a yell that scared the bejesus out of the boys around me. They jumped up and grabbed for their guns. It was all I could do to settle 'em down afore one of 'em shot me.

"Boys," I says, "it's Scurry comin'." I don't know what else might'a cooled 'em down. I know I sure felt a whole lot better.

Scurry's men started comin' in during the middle of the night. Looked to me like there was about 800 of 'em. Thank God. A more beautiful sight I ain't never seen.

They was awful tired. Some of 'em just dropped in their tracks they was so exhausted. Jacob Iils, he comes over and sits by me, holdin' his shotgun 'tween his knees.

"Howdy, Ezra," he says. Jacob's from our little town. We didn't sign together, but I know'd Jacob since I was little.

"How ya doin', Jacob," I says.

"I'm a might winded," he replies, "what with ten hours of marchin'. Bad roads too. We had to drag all them cannon up over the pass. Mules couldn't pull 'em."

"That's a shame," I tells him.

"How was it yestiday?" he asks.

"A might bothersome," I says. "Musta been a thousand Yankees." I may have been exaggeratin' a bit. "They kept goin' round our flanks. Couldn't stop 'em. So we pulled back. Held 'em then."

Jacob bobs his head. He reaches in his pocket and gets out his clay pipe. "You got any tobaccie?"

"A bit," I say.

"Share?"

"I guess." I reaches into my sack and brings out a twist and bites off a bit. I hands it over to him. He looks at it kind of funny.

"Not very much here," he says, turning the tobaccie in his fingers.

"I ain't got much."

He gives me the eye and packs his pipe. Takes a twig and gets a light from the fire.

"Think the Yankees'll fight?" He blows out a stream of smoke.

"They sure did yestiday. Them boys are Pike's Peakers, I hears. Meanlike."

"Well, I'm sure lookin' forward to tomorrow."

I give him a nod and roll up in my blanket and close my eyes. Let him smoke his pipe and look forward to the mornin'. I ain't.

Chapter 56

The bugle shattered the cold still air of the Union camp. It was three o'clock in the morning on March 27. "Damn," John Chivington grumbled, as he prepared to respond to the bugle call summoning all the officers to the tent of Colonel John Slough.

Slough had arrived an hour before at Kozlowski's Ranch with seven hundred more men in addition to the three hundred he'd sent ahead. Fourteen hundred men in all were now gathered for the fight, which seemed inevitable.

Chivington had pulled back to Kozlowski's yesterday afternoon. His men had overwhelmed the water supply at Pidgeon's Ranch. He'd left behind the hospital and eleven wounded men. They had sent the prisoners back to Fort Union under guard.

Chivington buttoned his tunic tightly over the girth of his stomach. He bent over to pull on his boots and grunted at the effort. It made him sweat and a little light-headed, even in the cold air.

He lifted his 315 pounds off the creaking bed and went out into the night. Slough's tent was alight. Chivington was pleased with Slough's sense of urgency. As he walked, the snow crunched under his boots. It was a pleasant sound. Maybe he had been wrong in his estimation of the man.

"Begging your pardon, sir, I don't think that's a good idea," Chivington said.

They sat around a camp table with a map unrolled on it. A kerosene lamp held down one corner of the map, providing a flickering light. Four of the most senior company commanders sat further back. They kept to themselves. Smoking but attentive. Between the smoke and the fumes from the lamp, the tent was filled, giving it a gauzy air.

Chivington was red in the face and exerting a lot of will to contain his anger. John Slough was sitting back in his chair with the top buttons of his tunic undone. His course white undershirt showed the stains of rough travel. He had a satisfied expression.

"If you believe the Confederates have anywhere near the same number of men on the field as we do," Chivington continued, "it's foolish to divide your command."

Slough abruptly leaned forward in his chair and pointed his finger at Chivington. His eyes went hard. "Watch your tongue, Major." The edge of Slough's uniform swung down with his sudden movement. A brass button on the loose flap flashed in the light of the kerosene lamp.

"The Rebels are at Johnson's Ranch," Slough said. I don't know their disposition. So, we will make a reconnaissance in force into the pass. When we catch them tomorrow, you'll be in a position to take them from the rear."

Slough tapped his finger on the map, pointing to an area parallel to and above Johnson's Ranch. Glorieta Mesa. "There. It will take them completely unawares. Your four hundred troops. Total surprise. We can end the Confederate threat here and now." He tapped the map again. "We need to be aggressive and do the unexpected. It's how battles are won, Mr. Chivington."

Chivington glanced around the tent at the four captains in attendance. They would not meet his eyes. Cowards. Or idiots. He got up and straightened his uniform. He needed time to get control of himself. He coughed into his hand. Then he looked at Slough.

"Sir," he said, "what if the Confederates are no longer at Johnson's Ranch? What if they've moved forward?"

Slough's hand waved away the objection. He grinned at Chivington. "Then you will be in a position to support me, Major. With almost a thousand men, I can hold out for quite some time."

Chivington was growing agitated. He was having trouble suppressing his anger. He had never been able to abide fools. And he bridled at the exercise of an authority he didn't respect. He grasped his hands behind his back to still them.

"The route you suggest takes me onto the ridge above and parallel to the pass. It's quite steep. I may not be able to descend, sir."

"If you hear me engage, seek a way down. I'm confident a man of your ability can find one." A smirk twitched the corners of Slough's lips. His tone was edged with sarcasm. Chivington had to grit his teeth.

"And what if I'm attacked, sir?"

"You won't be."

"But, sir..."

"Enough, Mr. Chivington. I've made my decision. Now I need some sleep." He stood up in dismissal. "Be prepared to move out at 9:00 a.m."

Chivington started. What the blazes was this? Nine o'clock? How could he hope to catch the Rebels unaware at Johnson's Ranch? It was several hours march. "I can be ready to leave at daybreak, sir," he said.

"That is all well and good, Major, but my men need to get some rest. We've had a long march."

This was idiocy, Chivington thought. This man could lose the entire territory if the Confederates broke through his lines. Fort Union would be practically defenseless. He clamped his mouth shut, not trusting himself to speak again. He saluted and turned.

"Mr. Chivington, your map, sir," said Slough, rolling up the map and extending it in his hand. Chivington turned back and took it without a word. He walked out into the cold darkness.

The man's a total ass, Chivington thought. He brought his fist down against his thigh in exasperation.

He was distracted for a moment by the moonlight. He noticed his footprints in the snow. How clear they were.

Nothing else was. If this goes wrong, he thought, he'll blame me for not coming to his support. They'll court-martial me. He thought of his wife. She had been against his enlistment. Now she would be humiliated. What can I do?

It was a good question.

Chapter 57

We was up early. Rolled outa my blanket and took a swig of water. At least it weren't snowin'. Clear and cold.

This ain't Texas, what with all these mountains and such. I guess that's all right. I could sorta like 'em if it weren't for this dang war. Maybe I'll come back here after. Practice law.

The fire was all burned down to cold ash. It was the usual with me, sratchin' at myself till I drew blood. These damn lice just don't go 'way. I think maybe they gotten into my beard.

We looked a sight, faces streaked with dirt and gunpowder. Weren't no water for washin'. My hand was hurtin' but I got no time to think on that. Don't hurt too bad anyway. Maybe I should see a doc after this fight.

Billy Dask, he come amblin' by. "Howdy, Ezra," he says. "You got any extra powder. Mine got all wet."

I shook my head and says, "Nope" and he wanders off. Billy ain't the most careful man. Gonna get hissself killed one of these days.

Twitchel still ain't come home and I'm starting to worry. Been lookin' for that dog for two days now. He ain't ever been gone this long. Not that I care. It just ain't a good omen. Damn dog.

I started me a small fire and cooked a little corn mush for breakfast. It didn't take long to make. Didn't take long to eat neither. As I was chewin', I started thinkin' on things.

It were right strange. Nothin' seemed to exist 'cept this sky and this camp. And the fear of getting shot. We got no mail, no newspapers. There was always rumors. Most of 'em wasn't true.

What was happenin'? Was we winnin' the war? How was Becky? Was she waitin'? I shook all that thinkin' aside. My head weren't made for it. Better to make sure my skin were in one piece.

These Yankees sure do confuse me. We expected 'em to attack yestiday. Set ourselves up in a good defensive position and waited all day. But it were dead quiet. You'da thought with all them men, they would'a attacked. We should send 'em a thank you or somethin'.

Today, crack of dawn, Scurry, he orders us to pack up all the rations we had into our sacks. Mine weren't too heavy, 'cause there weren't much food. Told us we was going to go to the Yankees if they wasn't coming to us.

Said March 27 was going to be a big day in Confederate history. Boys and me, we don't care all that much about history. We'd rather have a good breakfast.

Can't say I was looking forward to this march. My shoes done give out. My feet had sure gotten tender from wearin' boots. The ground was cold as hell. I shifted back and forth from foot to foot. Guess I got to find me some Yankee shoes that'll fit. Maybe some of them miniballs too. I been wantin' to try out my new rifle. Left it here today in one of the wagons.

Scurry says the supply wagons is to stay put. Officers sure got to think of lots of stuff. We ain't goin' that far and everythin' we got that ain't on our backs is in 'em. Got all our blankets, ammunition, and what food we has. Not enough of any of 'em. Don't want no stray cannonball doing us bad. Things is bad enough now.

I packed my stuff up pretty quick, took a piss in the latrine and thought I should check up on Walter. Walter, he ain't doing so good lately. I walked over to him. He was sittin', but his head was hangin' down. I squinched down beside him.

"Walter, how you doin'?" I says. Walter, he looks up. His eyes look funny.

"I don't feel so hot, Ezra. Weak and all. Cain't even hardly walk."

I leaned over and put the back of my hand against his forehead. Felt hot to me. "Looks like you got yerself a fever," I says. "You stay put. Rest some." I stood up. I was so stiff, I let out a groan. Must be getting old.

"You seen the doc?" I asks. He shook his head a little and it seemed like it hurt him. "You go on now and go see him. You tell 'em you need to stay behind today. I'll tell the First Sergeant."

There must be a hunnert or so others that's sick or wounded. At least Walter'll be safe, back here with the wagons.

"Come on, Davis." First Sergeant comes amblin' up. He jerks his thumb behind him towards the road. "Both of you." I go up and tell him Walter got hisself a fever and is real sick.

He looks at me queer like but don't say nothin' about Walter. "We ain't got all day," he says to me real hard. "You get into line." First Sergeant must'a slept bad. Well he ain't the only one, I can tell you.

Us boys, we took off at a pretty good pace, me steppin' real tender. Hoped we didn't have to go too far. On t'other hand, I could put off getting shot at for a while. It was good to get away from that camp. Smelled awful. At least the air smelled clean out here.

Wind nipped at my bare skin through my ragged shirt. So cold it give me goose bumps.

The sound of all the boys marchin' and the artillery grinding up ahead on the snow-covered trail was real loud. I couldn't hear myself think. I don't guess we was makin' more noise than usual. Must a-been the steep canyon walls that made it sound so loud.

My hand was hurtin', but I tried to ignore it. Pyron, he rides by, going in front like always. Smiles as he comes upon us and takes off his hat. Waves it and yells somethin' I didn't rightly hear.

About a mile along, we come upon Twitchel. He were beside the road. Dark brown stained his fur. Look to be a hole blown clear through his little body. It were a bullet, not a shotgun. Who would'a done somethin' like that?

I musta got a piece of dirt in my eye. Damn Yankees.

Chapter 58

He sat astride his big, gray-dappled mare, its rough coat ill-kempt. The mouth of a narrow side trail cut into the main road. Chivington's massive bulk was a rock to the soldiers tramping past, turning into the trail. His bearded face was ruddy from the cold wind.

Chivington tugged his big gold watch out of his pocket. The one his congregation had given him when he went off to fight. He held it up and moved it away from his face to get the numbers in focus. His eyes weren't what they used to be. It was almost noon. Yes, noon, he thought with a touch of anger.

He stuck the watch back into his pocket and spurred his horse to the front of the line of men. He was nursing a pain in his back that had been getting worse since last night. Maybe it was just nerves. He got that way before a battle. Chivington bit against his lip to distract himself.

The sun was bright without giving any warmth. It made the water that had frozen in the ruts of the road glitter in the snow. There wasn't any mud. At least that was good, but you had to be careful not to slip.

His column of four hundred Union troops had just past Pigeon's Ranch. There had been no sign of the Rebels but Chivington had no doubt they wouldn't just stay put waiting for Slough. The damn fool, he thought, his lips retracting into a scowl. This was going to be a disaster.

The snow was thin but hung on desperately in the sunshine as if daring the sun to take it. Enough snow to dampen the sounds of war. Chivington had reined in at the side of the trail and turned his horse to watch his men pass. As the sheep pass under the staff, he thought.

The narrow side path had a disused air. Brush intruded, giving it a ragged appearance. The men backed up, shuffling, as the line of two abreast gave way to a single file. Young men bumped and shoved. Spirited men. Men of whom Chivington was proud.

Some laughed and chewed tobacco. Spat. Some walked in silence, meditating what was to come. A soldier marching by looked up and said "God bless you, sir." Several others echoed the phrase.

Chivington straightened slightly in his saddle and a smile twitched at his lips. A bit of wind took a corner of his riding cloak back, displaying a flash of blue.

He lowered his eyes to focus on another young man who had spoken and Chivington touched his hat. The boy had a thin face and a prominent nose. There were smallpox scars on his cheeks.

He wondered if the boy would live through the day or if he would recognize him if he didn't. Why did they all rush to volunteer? It couldn't be slavery. No man would sacrifice his life for emancipation except maybe some of those fools up in Massachusetts. Certainly no one from Colorado. Perhaps it was the adventure, the comradeship, that made them feel so alive. What a paradox, this adventure with death.

He thought of his own son in Denver, not two years younger than that one. What was he doing? Would he run off to war too? Please God, let it be over before he gets to be of age, he thought. Then he grimaced.

The two field howitzers groaned against their limbers as they made a turn, the horses straining at the sudden shift in weight. Snow padded the sound of hooves against the earth.

The caisson kicked a stone. It hit his mare on the leg and she whinnied and moved fretfully under Chivington. "Easy girl," he said leaning and patting the horse's shoulder. "Easy."

Chivington watched as the men started to climb the trail as the canyon deepened below. The wind rustled the pine trees and the cold caused the men's breath to haze the air. They were in a good mood, laughing and chatting, unaware of the strategic blunder Slough had made.

He sat there on his mare, his dark eyes remote. Chivington's face was set and his muscles burned but he didn't move. The men thought he had a martial air. His calm presence was reassuring. What a splendid officer, a soldier thought as he went past, feeling proud that he was in his regiment. An officer rode by and saluted.

Chivington had a sudden fierce thirst. He started to reach towards his canteen. Then his hand stopped. He didn't want to do anything so ordinary. Not in front of boys who might die in battle that day. They needed to have someone more than an ordinary man in command.

He felt ponderous and slow, unable to respond but feeling like a pawn to be sacrificed. It wasn't his nature and that only made it worse.

The colors seemed washed out, the men, the landscape. It was the silence. There was the tramp of men, their jostling, their noise. But more. Overreaching it all was the silence made of the wind in the pines and the vast reaches of the mountains. And the silence, in its own way was more frightening than the snap of a musket, for it contained the unknown.

He had always been a man of action. If challenged, he confronted. He almost always won. But this wasn't a pulpit and he reckoned the Lord's ways were unknowable. He fingered the well-worn leather of the Bible he carried in the pocket of his cloak and recited the Lord's Prayer silently. Please God, let these boys be in your keeping.

Now he could only wait. The thought unbalanced him and he swayed slightly before catching himself. How could a man of the church, a man who knows the truth, be caught up in some lawyer's lie?

Chivington's uniform seemed to stifle him. He had always liked the cooling wind, but the wind provided no comfort today. He looked off into the distance as if he were afraid that his boys would see the sickness in his eyes. His horse quivered as though it could feel Chivington's mood.

Maybe Slough was right. Maybe he would be lucky. Chivington could only hope. He had already prayed.

Then the line ended. One or two stragglers. He sat. Uphill, the forest absorbed the men almost sadly. He turned his horse towards the West and followed.

Chapter 59

Sergeant Joshua Egan was in the second company of the Colorado Volunteers, marching along behind the cavalry. Shambling more than marching, actually. His lanky frame easily bore the rucksack and his gun.

Nice not to have to force march at dawn. It had surprised him when they hadn't left 'til long after sunrise. More like mid-morning. But Colonel Slough knew what he was doing. They were an hour behind Chivington's regiment.

He was favoring his right foot. It had gotten bruised on a stone a few miles back. Sidestepping a mound of steaming horse dung in the snow on the wide trail, he thanked his lucky stars it wasn't hot and dusty. Cold was a long-sight better, at least in his view.

He'd had a lot of heat and dust in his summers on the farm in Colorado. Never could get used to it, like his brothers. There'd been three of 'em. Two older. Seven kids in all. Let's see. He was twenty-one now. His oldest brother must be around thirty, he thought. Married, with two kids of his own.

His pa worked the farm. The kids worked too. Never had no schooling. They worked hard. Six hundred dry acres. Always just barely making it. Always hungry. His Ma was beyond caring. Worn out with work and children. Died in '60.

His Pa got angry when he volunteered. Complained. Who was going to do the work? Joshua didn't rightly care. He was excited. He deserved to have some fun. He liked being away from home. Away from his Pa.

Fun? He thought. It had been fun, sorta. Camping out and clowning with his friends. Drinking and playing cards. Even the chance of women, although he'd been too afraid to go with his friends.

Never shot no one. Now he was going into battle. He'd heard you were supposed to hate the enemy. He didn't feel anything. Maybe that was bad.

"When you think we'll find them Rebs?" Joshua said to the man walking beside him.

The soldier shook his head and moved his rifle to the other shoulder. "Don't rightly know. Soon, I 'spect."

Sooner than they might have thought. At that moment, a mile down the road beyond Pidgeon's Ranch, a unit of Confederate cavalry heard and felt the certain sounds of a major force in front of them.

They withdrew noiselessly into the woods and rode back to William Scurry and the main Texas force. The cavalry officer and Scurry talked in low voices as if someone could overhear. Other officers shushed their men instinctively.

The cavalry officer turned and motioned to his men. They dismounted to fight in the line. Carbines were pulled from their saddle sheaths.

Field guns were unlimbered and pulled into place. Drovers walked alongside the horses that were pulling the guns, quieting the beasts and minimizing the noise.

The cold wind was blowing in their faces. Noise wouldn't travel. But there was no sense in taking risks. The infantry, under Scurry's watchful eye, spread quietly out in a single file line of battle across the Santa Fe Trail. Skirmishers moved out to the right and left into the trees.

The pine woods were dense. Unless a man was moving, he couldn't be seen from twenty feet. The hills rose gradually on the sides of the main trail, then ascended steeply as they neared the mountains. Large rocks dotted the hills. The afternoon of the day lay undisturbed.

Chapter 60

Boom of a cannon liked to scare me out of my boots, 'cept I ain't got no boots no more. I was nice and comfy behind the rock off in the woods the right side of the trail, where Scurry done put me.

Waitin' and I must'a got sleepy, what with wakin' up all night. Had to jumped a foot. "Woo eeye," shouted one of the boys and took a shot with his musket. Didn't hit nothin'.

I peeked out over my rock careful like and I see Union cavalry skedaddle back up where they come from. Well, it wouldn't be long now. I scratched at myself.

Looked up at the sky. Clear day, though right cold, what with the rags on my back and no cloak. Had my blanket wrapped round me. We was a sorry bunch.

Must'a been near noon. Maybe a little past. I pulled out my stick of dried pork and started gnawin' on it. Figured as how there wouldn't be much time later on. Made me thirsty. I lifted my canteen and took a big swallow. They give us a bit of whiskey last night. I saved some and put it in my water. Tasted dandy.

No more than half an hour when all of the sudden hell broke loose on the other side of the line. Shootin' an' hollerin'. Went on quite a while. I were pretty scared I tell ya, but it was quiet on this side. Then there were a lot of Rebel yells, so it seemed as how it must'a been okay.

The Lieutenant, he rode past and I asked him what happened. Seemed a bunch of Yankees had tried to sneak down a ravine and turn our line, but we seen 'em and made short work of that bunch. 'Bout time our shotguns was good for somethin'.

Anyway, the Lieutenant said it was like shootin' fish in a barrel 'cause we was up high, shootin' down into the ravine and they got no place to run. Must'a killed seventy of 'em. Hope it's as easy over here.

Our artillery opens up on my side of the road. You could hear the balls whoosh overhead. Then the sounds changed. The shot whistled. I think they must'a been firin' grape-shot into the woods at the Yankee skirmishers. I seen grape-shot once when we was fooling around with the artillery boys in camp. It were a while back. My friend, he showed me a can filled with musket balls. Looked downright wicked.

I could hear branches snapping. Once in a while I heard a moan when some Yankee must'a got it. That's hard. Ain't nothin' you can do. Can't fight, nor shoot back.

Couldn't see nothin' from where I was. I wasn't too keen on poking my head out nowise. Figured someone would tell me when I was to move. If'n they forgot me, I wouldn't fault 'em none. I'm forgivin'.

Chapter 61

Colonel John Slough stood on a rise, several hundred yards behind the Union lines. He watched his Colorado boys move to the right and the left. He'd been surprised to find a Rebel force in his front. But he'd recovered his poise. Must be an advance party. His cavalry hadn't been sure how big the force was.

A double enveloping maneuver had worked for Chivington yesterday at Apache Canyon. He didn't see any reason it wouldn't work again. He looked martial in his tailored uniform with his aides coming and going, whispering a few words to a nod and a quick salute.

Until the Rebel cannons opened up. Then the sound of shotguns and that awful Rebel yell. Something was wrong.

The word of the massacre of Lieutenant Kerber's company in the ravine shook Slough. He'd sent Kerber to flank the Rebels and harass their artillery. It was brilliant. Now he had a disaster on his hands.

His Union troops were being pushed back. No rout yet, but his double enveloping maneuver had failed utterly. If the Texans attacked now, his lines were in disarray and his left flank was exposed. He had to do something.

If the Rebels broke through, Gabriel Paul would skewer him for assuming his command. Yes, he'd stretched Colonel Canby's orders a little to move forward on the offensive, but he was between the Confederates and Fort Union. He felt a wave of panic.

But it was the right thing to do. You couldn't just sit there on the defensive. His mind reeled. If he lost, they'd ruin his career. His reputation. They were just waiting.

His hands were sweating even though the day was cold. He called out to his aides. The sound of his voice startled him. He needed to calm himself. He concentrated as his aides gathered to him.

"I want to fall back into a defensive position." He spoke quickly with a slightly high voice. "The Confederates outnumber us." He didn't know that for a fact. "They're too well entrenched." That he did know based on the reports flooding in from the left and right. One of his aides nodded.

"Have the men retreat to Pidgeon's Ranch," he said. We can take advantage of the buildings and walls." He had to hold on. It was his only hope. That damn Chivington would stab him in the back.

"Yes, sir, it's a good position. We can use that low ridge to the South," one of his officers said. "It commands the road and the ranch."

"Good. Send all four of our mountain howitzers up there with two companies of troops. I want the rest of the artillery positioned on the left side of the road where they can get at the Rebel artillery if they attack."

He was starting to feel more in control. He straightened his back. "We need to hold our position until Major Chivington attacks. He'll come when he hears the cannons. Once the Rebels start to respond, we'll move to the offensive."

Chivington had better come, he thought. That damned man had better come. The thought that he might be able to blame Chivington flitted across his mind.

He mounted and rode back to Pidgeon's Ranch. The forward elements of his men were already being placed behind the adobe walls. He could see Union men wresting the field howitzers up the slope to the plateau above the ranch.

Joshua Egan cursed as his hand slipped on the rope. His palm burned. He didn't have any gloves. The gun he was hauling at slipped a few more feet down the hill before he could stop it. "Damn you," the Lieutenant called out. "Pull. We got to get this field piece into action." The four men pulling on the ropes ignored him.

John Chivington had proceeded four miles along the ridge that bordered the Apache Canyon. He rode again at the head of his column.

It was a beautiful scene. The air was clear and the conifers surrounding them swayed in a gentle wind with a delicate rustling sound.

The sun was lower in the sky casting ragged shadows in the forest.

It was silent. Silent in a strange way. Four hundred armed men were proceeding to try to kill as many other men as possible. But their noise was isolated, absorbed in a broader silence.

He had no intelligence, no knowledge of the enemy's dispositions. But the pain in his back had eased a bit. He felt more focused.

They had cut off the side trail about half a mile ago and the men were moving more slowly now as they broke a new trail. He had flankers out to the sides of his column and a group of men in front scouting and clearing the way. He wouldn't be surprised by the Rebels. At least that was past.

He had made the decision to leave the existing trail because he couldn't risk engaging a force coming to the support of the Confederates on the main trail. His job was to attack the rear of the Rebel forces at Johnson's Ranch. He couldn't risk being delayed. It had been a constant worry.

He was still a mile inland from the edge of the canyon, but he had been alert to the possibility of cannon fire. Muskets were too small to be heard at this distance. Thank God everything was quiet. Maybe the Rebels had fallen back without a fight. Or maybe Slough was taking his time.

It was a quirk of the terrain that the steep sides of the canyon enclosing the Santa Fe Trail thrust the booming sounds of the cannon straight up. A quirk that would have a profound effect on the Battle of Glorieta Pass. Chivington continued on towards what had been the Confederate rear with his mind at ease.

Chapter 62

Now there was nothing at all but rocks and sagebrush. There were no landmarks. Major John Chivington had no idea where they were. He was sweating under his uniform, although it was very cold. Not fear. He was anxious.

He hated to rely on guides he didn't know. Chavez, the leader of the New Mexican Volunteers, looked shifty to him. And that man, Anastasio Duran, who Chavez had said knew this mesa like the body of his own wife, seemed unsure and tentative. Well, thank the Lord that Slough was not engaged yet. He would have heard the cannons.

He was having trouble keeping his concentration. His back was hurting again. Every step his horse took sent a shooting pain down his leg.

A rider came on at a gallop and reigned in sharply. "Major Chivington," Manuel Chavez said, a look of excitement playing on his face, "we've found the Confederate baggage train. It appears to be almost undefended."

"Where?" said Chivington. A Godsend. But it seemed too good to be true. A trap? Who would leave their train unguarded? It would be fool-hardy.

"The enemy is camped at Johnson's Ranch."

"Mr. Chavez, did they see you?"

"Never," Chavez's voice was sharp. Who did this man, Chivington, think he was? "We saw them from our concealment at the top of the mesa."

"How long will it take to bring the men up?" His four hundred men were stretched out over a mile behind him.

"Perhaps an hour. It is not very far."

Chivington turned in his saddle towards his aide. A star-burst of pain caused his mouth to tighten. He stifled a cry, but he spoke sharply. "Lieutenant, please advise the officers to move the men quietly, but quickly, to my position forward.

"I desire the captains of A and B Companies", he continued, "to join me. Please advise all officers that silence is required. Halt the men three hundred yards to my rear. Order them to not speak or make any sound. We will be near the enemy. I will proceed forward with Mr. Chavez."

They were at the edge of a steep mesa, about 400 feet above the canyon floor. The entire Confederate baggage train was spread out below. Eighty or ninety wagons. They had been on the edge of the mesa for an hour, observing. It was mid-afternoon.

"Sir, they only have one cannon and about fifty men. Shouldn't we attack?" The commander of Company A was anxious. They had become aware of cannon fire in the distance, off towards Pigeon's Ranch. But that made no sense to Chivington. Slough was supposed to attack the Texans here. It could still be a trap. Best be sure. He didn't like being pressed.

Another half hour passed. The cannon fire seemed to getting more distant. The Texans below were milling around without purpose. There seemed to be no more of them, nor was there any sign of an ambush. Finally, he made his decision.

"Captain Lewis," Chivington said, turning to the commander of Company B, "I want you to determine how to get down this mesa as fast as possible and lead the troops in the attack. You will need to attack that six-pounder first," he said, pointing toward the Confederate cannon. It was an obvious point. "I will remain in this position to oversee the fight."

Twenty minutes later Chivington's entire command swarmed over the lip and down from the mesa. Four hundred men went pitching down the hill, slipping and cursing. They generally were trying not to fall on their face, raising all hell with their Indian war whoops. The Texans below were shocked, then they were terrified. Men ran in every direction seeking cover.

The advancing troops ran head-long into the Confederate battery, but the Texans got off only two rounds before the gunners broke and ran at the onslaught of Captain Lewis's men. The few Confederate defenders were overwhelmed and quickly captured.

In a battle frenzy, the Union soldiers tore into the wagons, looting them of wine and liquor, blankets and anything else of value. After the officers finally regained control, the cannon was spiked and anything that would burn was set to fire. Explosions from burning powder could be heard for miles.

Either it had been a God-given miracle, or an incredible stroke of luck. The action, small as it was, made John Chivington a hero and changed the war.

Chapter 63

"Captain," Slough said, concentrating fiercely to keep his voice flat, "send three patrols to find Major Chivington. Request that he return promptly."

"Where is Major Chivington, sir?"

"How the blazes should I know? He was to proceed up the left side of the canyon on the Glorieta Mesa. Flank the Rebels. But he has been gone for over four hours. Just find him!"

The captain left running, gesticulating to a soldier nearby.

"Sir," a lieutenant said, coming up on Slough's left, "we have placed men behind the walls and buildings throughout the perimeter of the ranch. We have good cover and the ability to quickly move men to support other areas." Slough grunted.

"I want our cannon massed in the center, there, behind that wall." Slough said, pointing. "They will cover the road. Send seventy of your best skirmishers into the hills on each side to assure we don't get flanked again." The lieutenant saluted and walked quickly away.

The problem Slough faced was that the Rebels had 500 more men in the field than he did. Men he had sent away. It allowed the Confederates to move men to either or both sides of his force to threaten to surround or enfilade him.

They had been doing it all day, which had precipitated the retreat back to Pigeon's Ranch. By withdrawing to the ranch, he massed his men and presented a stronger front. But he also subjected them to concentrated cannon fire and more open ground for the Rebels to maneuver. It was a desperate gamble. If they broke through, Fort Union would be open to them.

William Scurry had also used the time to reorganize his Texans. He planned a coordinated three-prong assault on the Union position. At two o'clock, he attacked.

Joshua Egan was behind a rock. It wasn't a particularly big rock, but it was the biggest he could find in the brush-covered foothills up to the left of Pidgeon's Ranch. He could see the road below.

The Union soldiers were pushing the big guns into the center behind the adobe wall at the edge of the ranch. He felt exposed out here. There were seventy other men, but they were scattered along the hillside. It was quiet and he waited. He was cold.

At two o'clock all hell broke loose. It looked to Egan like the entire Confederate army rose up about 600 yards from the ranch. A Rebel screech pierced the air and a gun behind the wall belched a gout of flame. Joshua hoped it was a ranging shot because it fell far short of the emerging ragged line running towards the ranch. He saw the ball bounce almost in slow motion and hit harmlessly against a stone beside the road. He was surprised when the stone exploded into shards.

That was his last chance to take a long look. The hillside below him blossomed with Rebels. He waited, holding his breath, as they advanced slowly towards him.

A Rebel fell with a scream, clutching at his stomach. Ezra Davis dived for the sparse cover on the hillside. No more than a bush. He felt feverish. His hand was hurting something fierce. The pain had gotten steadily worse. There were two companies of Texans on the left. An equal number on the right. If they could get to the top of the hillside, they could fire down into the ranch and make it hot for those blue-bellies. But they had to get up there. His lieutenant screamed for them to advance. Ezra struggled to his feet, but his leg gave way and he went to a knee as a ball sniped over his head. He struggled to rise again and started to stagger forward. He was having trouble focusing.

The Rebels were now one hundred yards away and struggling to run up the steepening hillside. "Fire!" yelled the Union lieutenant and

Joshua pulled the trigger on his musket. The musket kicked back into his shoulder like a mule. Black smoke covered the hillside. Joshua grabbed his ramrod and tore open the paper cartridge case with his teeth. He knew he had to reload quickly or he would die. He had never been more afraid.

Twenty boys fell in the firestorm that engulfed them. Ezra had fallen to the ground. He struggled to get up as the remaining Confederates rose to advance. He couldn't seem to make his legs work. He wanted to get up. He wanted to move. He passed out.

The next Union volley ripped a hole in the center of the slowly advancing line of Rebels. The Union lieutenant yelled, "Fix bayonets!" Then "Charge!" Seventy Union boys, yelling curses at the Rebels, charged downhill into the Confederates. Six men fell as the Rebels knelt to open fire.

Joshua looked into the terrified eyes of a young boy as he thrust his bayonet into his chest. The boy screamed as blood exploded. Joshua thought he was going to be sick, but he pulled his bayonet free in time to deflect a blow from a big Rebel and bring his rifle butt up under the boy's chin. It was pure reflex. He heard the bones crack. Then everything went quiet, except for the whimpering of the wounded.

Joshua sank to his knees, struggling to breathe. He lifted his head to see the rest of the Confederates running downhill. He was too tired even to lift his musket. In any event, it was unloaded.

On the road below, a thousand Confederates ran screaming towards the wall of Pidgeon's Ranch. Colonel Scurry was in front, turning back to urge on his men forward with a wave of his arm. At three hundred yards, Slough's massed artillery belched and a hail of canister tore into his line. Then another. Yet another. Scurry called the retreat. He was furious. He had to get to those guns. It was three o'clock.

The next attack took place thirty minutes later. The flanks held again and the main assault was again repulsed by a thunder of canister.

"Major Pryon," Scurry said. "Those guns are too strong. We just can't get at them. I want you to take 400 men and attack on the left. We have to break those Yankees on the flank. I'll feint towards the front to draw their attention. You must succeed." Scurry was grim and determined. "I will, sir. Thank you," Pryon said.

At 5 o'clock, the Rebels attacked again. Joshua Egan was so weary he could hardly lift his gun. My God, there were so many of them this time. He thought they had shot them all.

Hundreds of men advanced up the hill. This time they came in waves, one kneeling and firing, the other advancing. It was worth his life to even see down the hill. He scrambled back a few yards to another bush. Everyone was moving.

The casting of musket balls is not a precise art. The one that killed Joshua Egan was just a tiny bit heavy. At one hundred yards, it dropped a quarter inch more than it should have. It was not even aimed at him. It was aimed at a soldier crossing two yards behind him and caught Joshua on the cheek, below his left eye, as he rose to fall back again. If he hadn't risen at that moment or had the ball been lighter, he would have lived. It was a random act of war.

Ezra Davis awoke to the renewed shooting. But his vision was blurred. He felt as if he was burning up. He struggled to a knee. "Come on, Ezra Davis," he muttered to himself, "you ain't no coward." He blacked out again.

"Sir," a captain said, approaching Colonel Slough and saluting. He was being deliberate, but he was clearly anxious. "Our left flank is buckling. There are just too many Rebels."

"Damn it. This can't be happening," Slough said striking his fist in his palm.

"Sir, it is happening. What are your orders?"

"I don't know. Give me a moment." Damn Chivington. Where was he? Why didn't he attack? This was his fault.

"There is little time, sir. I doubt that the men can hold out for another half hour."

"What would you suggest, Captain?" He stared into the man's eyes. His jaw was clenched.

"Sir, we could send Major Benning's battalion to support our left flank."

"But that would expose our center."

"We would have to withdraw, sir. But it would be an orderly withdrawal, not a defeat."

"Very well." Slough seemed to shake off his uncertainty. He spoke in a decisive voice. "Give Major Benning the orders to deploy his battalion to support our left flank. We will retreat to the narrowest part of the Trail between here and Kozlowski's Ranch. Get me a map."

A map was produced. Slough pointed at a place on the Santa Fe Trail approximately two miles beyond Pidgeon's Ranch. "We'll regroup here. We can secure our flanks against the sides of those steep ridges. I believe we can hold." But could he?

"Yes, sir."

"I want the withdrawal by battalions. The guns shall remain until we have withdrawn. Wesley's battalion will remain in support of the guns. When the rest have withdrawn, Major Wesley and Major Benning will provide the rear guard. Give the orders immediately."

It might work. But to plan new defenses without any preparation was an enormous risk. Slough knew it. But what could he do? How could things have gone so wrong?

It was dusk, quickly turning to night. Colonel William Scurry's Confederates had occupied Pidgeon's Ranch. Scurry had set up his headquarters in the main ranch house. A fire was burning. A bottle of whiskey was open on the table in front of Scurry.

Scurry felt the glow of another victory. He occupied the field. But it was growing dark. His men were exhausted. He needed time to reorganize and plan the next phase of his attack. He felt confident he would succeed. The Yankees were bloodied and disheartened.

He turned to Major Charles Pryon. "A tremendous victory, Charles. You should be pleased."

"I am, sir. Shall I organize the men to pursue?"

"No, Charles, I think not. Not tonight. We need to resupply and regroup. The wounded need to be attended to. The morning will be soon enough. I think we can give the men a night's rest. Please have the supply train brought forward. And send a man to the blue-bellies extending a truce until 8 o'clock in the morning."

It was then that a rider galloped into the ranch house yard and burst into the room. "Sir," he said. "There is a glow in the West. It appears to be a fire of some sort. There is a concern that it may threaten our baggage train."

Both Scurry and Pryon rushed to the door and peered at the glow in the darkening sky. "May we send a company to investigate?" the rider asked with anxiety in his voice.

"Immediately, man. Send two companies. I want you to do what is necessary to secure our wagons. Go quickly."

Only it was too late.

Chapter 64

SANTA-FE GAZETTE.
SANTA FE NEW MEXICO MARCH 30 ,1862
VOLUME 4 | NUMBER 8

On Saturday, the 29th the enemy retreated to Santa Fe. They began to arrive in the afternoon in squads of different sizes and continued to come in until a late hour Sunday morning. Their appearance clearly manifested the severe usage to which they had been subjected. Some rode, some walked and some hobbled in. All were in the most destitute condition in regard to the most common necessities of life. None the less, by the order issued by Col. Scurry of the Confederate Army, it will be seen in what light he regarded the battle of Pigeon's Ranch which he calls the battle of Glorieta Pass. We have frequently heard the remark made by military men after a successful battle that they could not stand another such victory.

Soldiers – I am proud of you
Go on as you have commenced,
and it will not be long until
not a single soldier of the United
States will be left upon the soil
of New Mexico

Chapter 65

April 4, 1862
(A letter unsent, later discovered in Santa Fe)

Dear Sophie,

I have had no quiet nor the time to write for the past week. We remain here in Santa Fe even as the Confederates seem to have suffered a great defeat. There is no order. Hundreds of wounded boys have been carried or have dragged themselves in, many in rags. Their wounds are dreadful.

No one has a rucksack. How did they eat? And there are no baggage wagons. Not one returned from the battle. I have never seen an army without its baggage train.

We learned there were men who had been left behind. I found an old farm wagon and the oldest mule I have ever seen. We women had to go out from Santa Fe. We could get no one else to go. Many boys who were too broken to walk, were left by the side of the road.

We drove out in the freezing wind. There were vultures everywhere among the bodies of those poor boys. They had bloody beaks. Sometimes a shred of torn skin was hanging from them. They even were feeding off boys who were still alive, though barely so. It was a terrible sight. I will see those black flat eyes in my nightmares.

If we came to a boy and he was alive, we would try to get him into the bed of the wagon. It was high. Two small women had to lift him. It was difficult to be gentle.

The bed of the wagon was small, so we could take only a few of them until we had to go back. Each trip from Santa Fe was more difficult. Each took more time since we had to go farther and farther.

I have made eight trips in the last three days. There are now only the dead left on the road to Santa Fe.

Forgive me, but I must write about this or I fear I shall be overcome. They have set up a tent for operating. Those whom the doctors think too severely wounded are left outside to die on the cold ground. Some are the ones we brought in. The others are taken into the tent.

There is a long wooden table. A boy is hoisted upon it by two men. A surgeon, in a bloody apron, with his knives and saws stands over him and saws or cuts. The surgeons look like butchers with blood up to their elbows. It is done quickly, as it would be when butchering a cow. Blood runs freely off the sides of the table and soaks into the ground. The surgeons stand in mud made of dirt and blood.

There is no anesthetic. They give the boy a drink of brandy and a leather strap he can clench between his teeth. Some boys die of shock. The screams coming from the tent are beyond describing.

The old farm wagon I used waits at the door of the tent. Bloody arms and legs that have been sawed off are dumped into it. When it is full they drive it off somewhere. While it is gone, they pile more, bloody, severed arms and legs by the door.

The stench was awful at first. We have now grown used to the smell of death and festering wounds. Can it be God's will that we become immune to this horror?

And yet it is not the worst. The worst is the boys left outside to die. They try so hard to be brave. We do what we can for them. We give them water and hold their hand. We pray with them and try to make them feel cared for. The air is rent by boys crying to God to release them from their suffering. And so many die in our arms.

There was one boy, not yet eighteen, with a bloody wound in his side. We could not stop the bleeding. I was holding his head. He looked up at me with such wide eyes and got the most angelic look on his face. He murmured a blessing to me and passed on. I had to lean across him to close his eyes so that he might rest. To one side of the tent, still, stiff bodies lie in the snow, placed one next to the other, like logs.

It is so cold that several have frozen to death. There are not enough blankets. There are not enough beds. Only the sickest boys sleep indoors. It is a little warmer inside. The other wounded sleep in tents where twenty or more cots are set up cheek by jowl. We try to keep the tents clean, but there is filth everywhere. And we sit, talking to the boys to offer them prayer and hope. One of the boys, whose arm had been amputated, smiled at me and called me Ma.

I am so weary. I exist in a half-waking sleep. When I close my eyes, I am beset by nightmares. My hands tremble and I am unsteady. But I must go on.

I have spoken to Colonel Scurry about food for our boys. Without food, how will they survive? He is sympathetic, but there is none, or a very little. There is nothing he can do. He must also feed the other men and us as well.

We eat as the officers do. Dinner is a thin soup, almost without nourishment, two small corn cakes and a tiny piece of meat. What kind, I do not know nor do I care to ask. I save my corn cakes for the boys.

All of us have been treated as well as possible by the Confederate officers, and with all courtesy, even in these stressful times. We have, in our turn, done our best to succor the wounded.

Many of our tasks are disgusting. For example, we take turns emptying bedpans. The stench is quite awful, but it must be done. Even here, it is not easy for me. Yesterday, Abigail McKenna refused to take her turn. She says she will not do it. I am powerless to force her to do so and now all of the others of us must do more.

I have heard talk among the officers of a retreat from Santa Fe. There are dozens who cannot be moved. We will stay with them as long as possible, until we become a burden.

Sophie, you cannot imagine waking each morning only to find the days filled with suffering that you are helpless to change. And nothing but the same tomorrow and the day after that. It is more than I can bear, God help me.

Your loving sister,
Louisa

Chapter 66

"And exactly how do you propose we fight without food, sir? Without ammunition? You did not save a single wagon."

"General Sibley, our situation is unfortunate, but I am not responsible."

"And if not you, Colonel Scurry, then who? It was utter incompetence, man." Sibley banged a fist on the table. It made the glass of whiskey by his left hand tremble.

William Scurry was an erect man of forty with a long face and a full beard. He was standing. Sibley had not asked him to sit. His dark eyes under heavy brows were glowing with anger. Scurry's lips were so tightly compressed that his voice quavered. How dare this man speak to him in that manner.

"With all respect, General, I left three companies to protect the baggage train. They were positioned a quarter of a mile to the East of our wagons on the Santa Fe Trail. When we routed the Yankees and drove them back to Pidgeon's Ranch, Major Brassack chose to move his troops an equal distance forward so his reserve forces would be available to me, while continuing to place himself in a position to protect our supplies. Sir, even if Major Brassack had been there, he would have been overwhelmed. The Yankees had twice as many men, as well as the element of surprise."

William Scurry was weary. He had been everywhere, issuing instructions, visiting the wounded, gathering such food as he could to feed 1,300 men. All of their supplies had been destroyed in the baggage train. He would have to broaden the search for food. Further into the countryside. Heaven knows where they could find adequate ammunition. The brigade was in desperate shape. Santa Fe was stripped bare, as was everywhere else, but it wasn't his fault.

Sibley shook his head with a look of contempt.

"I do not fault Major Brassack," Scurry continued in the face of Sibley's look. "He made a tactical decision during the course of battle. It was a reasonable one. We had the worst of luck."

"I see. No one is to blame. You may have destroyed my campaign and rendered us unable to fight, and no one is to blame. I do not agree, sir." His voice almost mounted to a shout. Red started to suffuse his cheeks.

Scurry struggled to maintain his calm. It was difficult. He dug his nails into the hands clasped behind his back.

"General Sibley, no one could have predicted that the enemy would divide his forces in a manner that would deny him support. I would not. Nor that the enemy would discover our train and fall directly upon it before Major Brassack could return."

"I do not want your excuses, Colonel."

"Do you want my resignation, sir? If so, I will insist upon a court-martial to determine where responsibility lies. I would like to know, sir, what you would have done differently. If you had been in the field." General Sibley had arrived in Santa Fe only yesterday. He had never led his troops in battle. Damn it, he was a drunk. Everyone knew it.

"You are getting dangerously close to insubordination, Colonel Scurry. I suggest you choose your words carefully. And no, I do not wish your resignation. I want you to suffer the mess you have created."

Scurry did not trust himself to speak. He only nodded.

"What I do want you to do, Colonel, is to confiscate all the money in every bank and store in Santa Fe. We will need to buy supplies if we cannot take them. I will not give up our quest because of your failure. Do you understand me?"

"Yes, sir."

"Good. Scour this town and every ranch within five miles. Let us hope we can find what we need to sustain us. Dismissed."

Chapter 67

SANTA-FE GAZETTE.

SANTA FE NEW MEXICO APRIL 5, 1862

VOLUME IV | NUMBER 8

Public Money Seized

When General Sibley was in Santa Fe he issued an order for the seizure of all the funds in the Territorial treasury. The money was appropriated to the General's private use. This is a palpable violation of the rules of war.

Praiseworthy

The attention bestowed by some of the ladies of Santa Fe upon the sick and wounded Texans in the hospital in this city is worthy of the highest commendation. In health, the invalids were regarded as enemies; in sickness they were administered to in kindness that might have been shown to friends. The ladies most active in these Christian ministrations are Mrs. Canby, Mrs. Edgar, Mrs. Watts and Mrs. Chapin.

Chapter 68

SANTA-FE GAZETTE.

SANTA FE NEW MEXICO APRIL 9, 1862

VOLUME IV | NUMBER 8

Previous to the departure of the Union Army from the city they had concealed in a skillful manner all the goods intended for future distribution. Although the Texans suspected that government property of this character had been concealed and made frequent investigations in reference to it they failed to make the discovery until April 8. The place of concealment was undoubtedly revealed to them by some person who betrayed confidence which had been reposed in him, and thereby supplied them with blankets and other articles of which they were sorely in need.

Chapter 69

April 11, 1862
(Santa Fe, New Mexico)

My dear Edward,

I congratulate you on your victory and pray that you are well. Santa Fe is now deserted and the Rebels have fled to the South. You should know that we women were treated well by them, or as well as could be expected. It has been bitterly cold and food has been short. But we have fared on, as you would expect.

I hesitate to write this, but I must confess to you my wrong before you hear it from others. I know I have been willful and have not been a good soldier's wife. I have brought upon you criticism which has hurt your career. The scorn you must have suffered, and the whispers that you could not even control your own wife. Oh, I well know. It is a mark of how good you must be to have prospered so.

I have done something dreadful. So awful that you may not be able to forgive me. But please know, I could not bear the suffering. Boys not much older than our beloved Mary now would have been. They were broken and bleeding. Some without arms or legs. Starving and perishing with the cold. Dying. So many dying. I could not bear it upon my soul. I could not make any mother suffer as I did.

I showed them where you had buried food and blankets. There, I have said it. I am a traitor, although I do not feel it so. These starved boys were no longer a threat to you, or to our Union. They were just boys. If you could have only heard their cries. I can still hear them in my dreams. The Confederates did discover other military supplies buried close by. I did not disclose those supplies to them. But even so,

I would have done it.

Yes, I did betray you. I must live with that. But I did not betray you in my heart. I ask, I beseech you, Edward, to forgive me.

I love you,
Louisa

Chapter 70

SANTA-FE GAZETTE.

SANTA FE NEW MEXICO APRIL 9, 1862

VOLUME IV | NUMBER 8

Promoted

We now learn that Col. Canby has been promoted to the office of Brigadier General. This is an appropriate honor conferred upon an efficient and worthy officer of the army.

We have also learned, to our surprise, that Lieutenant Colonel John P. Slough of the Colorado Volunteers has resigned his commission. We find this puzzling given his great victory at Glorieta Pass.

Chapter 71

The Civil War Journal of the Millennium Group

The Confederate Army won a victory at the Battle of Glorieta Pass, but it was a pyrrhic victory. The destruction of the Confederate supply wagons was a disaster. The Confederates had won every significant battle in the campaign, but General Sibley was crippled without supplies. He could not decide whether to continue or retreat. Colonel Edward Canby's actions forced his decision.

Canby recognized the strategic impact of the Battle of Glorieta Pass and ordered his troops to march from Fort Craig and Fort Union to join at Albuquerque. They consolidated on April 13.

Out of supplies and ammunition, his rear threatened, Sibley chose to abandon his campaign and retreat. But avoiding Canby's pursuing troops proved to be a more difficult task.

The Union cavalry overran a small train of Confederate supply wagons at Peralta on April 14th and the sides formed for battle. Canby halted the attack before it began. It remains unclear why he did so. A blinding sandstorm that afternoon ended the encounter.

Sibley, hoping to avoid further battle, ordered his worn and haggard men to leave the Rio Grande and force marched them the last 100 miles through the Jornada del Mueurto desert, the Journey of the Dead Men.

Of the 2,500 men who invaded New Mexico in January 1862, 1,500 returned to Texas.

Chapter 72

April 16, 1862
(the field near Peralta)

My dear Louisa,

I have delayed in responding to your letter, as I did not know what to do or say. What you have written has occupied every waking hour not devoted to this battle, which continues even with the enemy in retreat.

I have always been determined to do my duty, as I perceived it, even in the face of possibly doing wrong. You have always been determined to do what is right, even in the face of possibly doing wrong. They seem so alike, but I see now how different they are. Perhaps God whispers to you. I pray that he does.

I know you so well. We have been through many years together. And we have known such sadness. You are a strong-minded woman. That has been both good and bad.

You could not see any boy suffer as those terribly wounded boys have. I, too, see our boys, whom I have sent into battle, come back rent and screaming. I feel it also, but I must shield myself so I can do my duty. You cannot. You could never.

I have come to realize I cannot judge you. So, yes, you did wrong. Those supplies comforted those who could still fight, as well as your wounded boys. The Texans might have surrendered, rather than retreat to fight again. Perhaps to do harm to our cause.

But you saw boys broken and torn apart. Who were starving. Who were freezing. You were there. I know, in your heart, they were your boys. You could no more let them suffer and die than you could let our beloved Mary suffer and die, if in any way you could have prevented it.

So, I say, if you did right in your own eyes, I will stand beside you and say so to whomever may ask.

> I shall, indeed, I must, remain your devoted husband,
> Edward

Chapter 73

"I were one of the lucky ones, ma'am," Ezra Davis said, replacing the old campaign hat on his head. He stepped back from the graves of Edward and Louisa and straightened. "General, sir. Ma'am."

—————————

He did an about-face and marched slowly into the gray Confederate sky.

Epilogue

Louisa Hawkins Canby

Louisa was never charged with treason. The Union victory at Glorieta Pass and the retreat of the Confederate Army from the New Mexico Territory seems to have washed away any memory of her action's, at least in Union minds.

Soon after Sibley's defeat, Louisa moved East with Edward. Only in 1864 was Edward again allowed to move from behind his desk to take command and participate in the impending defeat of the South. They found a new home in New Orleans.

Following the War, Canby was chosen to serve as military commander of several Southern districts. There, Louisa was known for her tendency to give away things to the needy wherever she went. "I can hardly keep anything, there is so much suffering about us," she wrote.

When Edward was appointed to command the Department of Columbia, including Oregon, Washington and Alaska, they moved to Portland. In 1873, after a year of war with the Modoc Indians, an unarmed Edward and several of his party were murdered during peace talks, by Captain Jack, a leader of the Modoc.

Louisa found her husband's death unbearable and became ill, rising from her bed only after a week. When the people of Portland learned of her scant pension from the Army (thirty dollars a month), they raised $5,000 and presented it to her as a gift. She was still beloved.

Henry Hopkins Sibley

Sibley's conduct of the New Mexico campaign led to charges filed by one of his officers. They were sent to the Secretary of War, but due to bureaucratic delays and illness, they were never thoroughly investigated. The charges ranged from cowardice to drunkenness to inhumane treatment of the wounded.

Sibley was called to Richmond where he conferred with Jefferson Davis. President Davis chose to dismiss the charges, based on affidavits from Sibley's loyal staff refuting the charges in detail.

Sibley was then ordered to resume command of his brigade in Louisiana and placed under the command of General Richard Taylor, the son of the former President of the United States.

The defeat of the Confederates at the Battle of Bisland resulted in the loss of the richest part of Louisiana to the South. On at least two occasions during the battle, amidst other tactical errors, Sibley disregarded Taylor's direct orders, devising his own plans with disastrous results.

Taylor concluded that Sibley's strikingly poor leadership contributed markedly to the rout, and said so in his official report. Shortly after the battle, Taylor preferred charges and ordered Sibley court-martialed, effectively ending his military career. Sibley was ultimately found not guilty by the court-martial board in a convoluted decision. Ironically, while Sibley was still seeking a new command, the Confederate Army in the Trans-Mississippi surrendered on June 2, 1865 to the Union commander, Edward R. S. Canby.

After Sibley signed his parole papers, he confronted his condition. He had no home, no land and no wealth. He was unemployed and unemployable. Although royalties on the widely used Sibley Tent amounted to more than $100,000, the government refused Sibley any compensation.

Sibley was destitute. But in 1869, he had a stroke of luck. The Khedive of Egypt was seeking Civil War veterans to reorganize the Egyptian Army. Sibley signed a five-year agreement. Vindication was at hand. Egypt was an exotic and glamorous place for the new Inspector-General of Artillery.

While Sibley was one of the first Americans to arrive in Egypt, he turned out to be one of the first to leave. His drunkenness was his undoing. His alcoholism had become severe, and the Khedive, tired of the problem, dismissed him in 1873.

In broken health and in poverty, Henry Sibley died in 1886, still hoping to collect the royalties on the Sibley Tent.

Edward R. S. Canby

Edward Canby spent more than a year in administrative positions in the East after the War. His strength was in organization and planning, not in fighting. Some questioned his tactics of minimal engagement in the New Mexico war, although the strategy was ultimately successful.

He was, however, appreciated. Canby was one of only ten brigadier generals retained by the Army following the end of the Civil War. Promoted to Major General, he commanded the Department of Columbia. While he was serving in the Pacific Northwest, the war with the Modoc Indians broke out. Fought to a standstill, the Army wanted to initiate peace talks. In 1873, during the talks, an unarmed Canby was killed by the Modoc leader, Kintpuash (known as Captain Jack). Canby had written of his doubts of negotiating with the Modocs. His major concern was that Captain Jack was so concerned about treachery (he had been told that the Governor of Oregon intended to hang him immediately after his surrender) that he might be capable of treachery himself. And so it was.

Canby's death shocked Washington. His colleague, William Tecumseh Sherman, then General of the Army, ordered a retaliatory raid against the Modoc. The raid effectively ended the Indian threat to Northern California and the California gold fields.

John Slough

Following the War and his resignation from the Army, Slough was named Chief Justice of the New Mexico Supreme Court by President Andrew Johnson. He was appointed to fight corruption and break down the system of patronage in the New Mexico courts.

His fiery temper led him to slander an enemy, William Ryerson, in public. Ryerson drew a gun and demanded that Slough retract his slander. Upon Slough's hot refusal, Ryerson fired. Slough died a day later. Ryerson was found not guilty at his trial although many thought the court proceedings were corrupt.

John Chivington

The fighting preacher was commanding the 3rd Colorado Cavalry in October, 1864. The Territorial Governor, John Evans, had offered protection to multiple Cheyenne and Arapaho chiefs in return for surrender and peace. The chiefs accepted and settled into the land.

After learning of the accord, Chivington complained to the head of the Department of Kansas, demanding that the agreement be abrogated. In his view, eradication was the only way to deal with the savages.

In November 1864, with 800 men, Chivington marched on the peaceful Indians. Since the tribes were at peace, most of the braves had been sent away to hunt. Chivington attacked on November 29th. His soldiers killed the majority of the Indians, mostly women and children, in what became known as the Sand Creek Massacre.

Chivington was condemned for his part in the massacre, but he had already resigned his commission. He became an unsuccessful freight hauler and something of a scoundrel. He died of cancer in 1894.

William Scurry, Thomas Green and Charles Pryon

Both William Scurry and Thomas Green were promoted to general officers in the Confederate Army and each died in battle in April 1864.

Charles Pryon became a colonel and led cavalry units throughout the remainder of the War. He retired to his ranch and died in 1869.

The Famous Historical Bit Players

Kit Carson

Kit Carson was one of the most colorful and legendary figures of the Old West. After the war, he led forces to suppress the Western Indian tribes by destroying their food sources. Carson was brevetted a Brigadier General and took command of Fort Garland, Colorado. He was there only briefly, as poor health forced him to retire from military life.

Carson was married three times and had ten children. He died on May 23, 1868.

In recent years, Kit Carson has also become a symbol of the American nation's mistreatment of its indigenous peoples.

William Becknell

In 1821 Becknell faced substantial debt. Under intense financial pressure, he left on an extended trading trip to hunt and trap for furs.

Becknell and his group reached Santa Fe in mid-November 1821, the first to establish a rough overland trade route between Missouri and New Mexico.

Four years later, he helped map the Trail. For his efforts in opening up an improved route for regular traffic and military movement, William Becknell became known as the Father of the Santa Fe Trail.

In 1835 Becknell sold up and moved on to Texas. During the Texas War of Independence, Becknell organized and led a cavalry unit, then briefly served as a Texas Ranger. He was elected as a member of the legislature in the newly established Republic of Texas.

Becknell died on April 30, 1865, in bed at home.

William Tecumseh Sherman

One of the foremost generals of the Civil War, Sherman's famous March to the Sea helped end the war. Sherman is still loathed by many Southerners today.

Sherman did not see action in the Mexican-American War, unlike many of his contemporaries. Instead, he was stationed in Northern California where he spent several years as an administrative officer, eventually rising to the rank of captain.

He resigned his commission in 1853, but remained in San Francisco with his growing family. Sherman became a banker, but his bank failed in 1857.

For several months, he worked as the president of a St. Louis streetcar company, but after the attack on Fort Sumter, his brother John secured him a commission as a colonel in the U.S. Army.

After the fall of Vicksburg July 4, 1863, President Lincoln recognized Sherman with a commission as a brigadier general of the regular army. Sherman assumed control of all Western armies when Grant was transferred East as commander of all Union forces.

As part of his strategic March to the Sea, Atlanta was nearly destroyed. Despite his earlier fondness for the South, his strategy of "total war" brought devastation to the region.

Sherman remained in the U.S. Army after the war. When Grant became president in 1869, Sherman assumed command of the United States Army.

He retired in 1884, eventually settling in New York and refused many who urged him to seek public office. "I will not accept if nominated, and will not serve if elected," he famously said.

Sherman died in New York on February 14, 1891, at age 71.

John C. Fremont

Called "The Pathfinder," Fremont was hailed as a great explorer of the West. Frémont was the son-in-law of a prominent politician, Sen. Thomas Hart Benton of Missouri.

With Sen. Benton's help, Frémont was chosen to lead an 1842 expedition to explore, with the guide Kit Carson, the area beyond the Mississippi River to the Rocky Mountains. While he did little original exploring, he did publish narratives and maps based on his expeditions.

Frémont then returned to California and became active in rebelling against Spanish rule and starting the Bear Flag Republic in northern California.

Settling in California, which by then had become a state, he briefly served as one of its senators. He became active in the new Republican Party and was its first presidential candidate, in 1856.

During the Civil War, Frémont received a commission as a Union general and commanded the U.S. Army in the West for a time. His tenure in the Army came to an early end when he issued an order freeing enslaved people in his territory. President Abraham Lincoln relieved him of command.

Frémont later served as the territorial governor of Arizona from 1878 to 1883. He died at his home in New York City on July 13, 1890.

Discussion Questions

1. With whom do you identify? Why?

2. Is there an inevitability in Louisa's actions?

3. It is not hard to understand Louisa's compassion to alleviate the suffering of the wounded Southern boys. Was she a heroine? Was she a traitor? A traitor is defined in law as one who gives aid and comfort to the enemy. Was she a moral person? Is morality a matter of short term and long-term consequences, or just those that are immediate?

4. Does it matter that her actions had a broader impact than helping the wounded? How many Union boys were killed by the Confederate troops who got away because they now had access to food and ammunition?

5. Why did Canby respond to Louisa's actions as he did?

6. Was Sibley incompetent? Sickly? Insecure? He certainly was an alcoholic and felt put upon during his entire career. But he invented the tent and stove used widely by the Army into World War One. Is insecurity the fuel of great achievements and talent the vehicle?

7. What is the role of God in war? Pastors on both sides cited the bible to prove God was on their side.

8. Was the North fighting to free the slaves or put down the rebellion of the Southern states? What role did economics play?

9. How does the revolt of the Southern states from the United States differ from the revolt of the colonies from the English?

10. Did the South win or lose the war?

In the Presidential election of 1876, Tilden, the Democratic candidate for President, won the popular vote. But the electoral vote was in dispute. Hayes, the Republican, made a deal with swing Southern states to become President. In return he withdrew all remaining Federal troops and return political control of the South to white Southerners.

The era of Jim Crow commenced. The rights of Blacks were repressed. For seventy years thereafter, the Democratic Southern voting block, known as the Solid South, controlled in Congress those issues its representatives deemed vital to Sothern interests, including Black voting and civil rights.

So, who really won the war?

Notes on Research

I'm a history buff, and as part of that, a student of the Civil War. I've read dozens of Civil War histories and biographies of Lee, Lee's lieutenants, Grant, Sherman and Lincoln, among many others

I knew the Civil War was fought from the Mississippi, east through the South, to the Atlantic Coast. Imagine how shocked I was to learn (by accident) about Sibley's Western campaign. And how intrigued I was about trying to recreate it, although I'm not sure a six-year endeavor is what I had in mind.

Research is one of the great pleasures of writing. And even a greater pleasure in writing a historical novel.

Apart from the obvious research into the lives of the main historical figures, including Louisa, Edward Canby and Henry Sibley, there was the infinitely harder job of trying to find the voice and motivation for each of these folks in the absence of letters and diaries. It took me a year of reading the diaries of Union and Confederate woman to find Louisa's voice in my head.

Then there were the places they lived. What was Monterey like in 1850? What was Fort Bridger or Santa Fe like? And, of course, there was the history of the Santa Fe Trail and William Becknell.

It was pretty straight forward to explore the battles in the Confederate campaign to capture the West. Those battles and all that went into them are part of history and fairly well documented. To paint a picture of them in my mind was more difficult.

I did extensive research on Union and Confederate armament. The Union development of the Minie ball was particularly interesting. The Minie ball was not a ball. It was a cast, hollow pointed, soft lead bullet. It slid easily down the rifled barrel of an Enfield musket. Rifling is the spiral etching inside a rifle barrel. It grips the bullet and causes it to rotate through the air. When fired, the Minie ball expanded to fill the rifling in the barrel, turning the bullet and greatly increasing accuracy and distance. There are about two sentences in the book as a result of that research.

I also learned what a caisson was and how it was an element of the artillery used by both sides. Those caissons actually did go rolling along.

As I wrote *The Whisper of a Distant God*, the research projects, greater and smaller, kept coming. But perhaps the most fascinating thing I discovered were the online archives of newspapers. They went back to before the Civil War. Real newspapers photographed and uploaded. I could read (and sometimes reproduce) how events were actually seen at the time.

The real danger, at least for someone like me, is that I get so lost in the research, I don't have time to write. I got lucky.

Acknowledgements

Of course, to Anne. She's the heart of everything I do.

And to her brother and sister-in-law David and Janet Cooper. They are my friends, which says a lot about how tolerant the family is. They read the manuscript and all the Questions for Discussion and gave me their thoughtful suggestions.

Micalyn Harris reads all my drafts. What stamina. And she knows stuff.

Harvey Champlin has been my friend for years, which is the only reason I can think of that he keeps coming back for more. Bless him.

Leslie and Tom Weinberger never fail to help and always give me the benefit of their insight in the most charitable way. After all, I'm sensitive. I was trained as a lawyer.

And to my buddy Clark Miller. This book really threw him. He couldn't hear my voice. Our forthright discussions really focused me. I realized I didn't want my voice to be heard at all. I wanted these people to tell this story in their own voices.

My thanks is not enough for each of them.

Made in the USA
Las Vegas, NV
27 April 2024